"Moving Up in the World, Aren't You?"

Darren asked, his tone as biting as his words.

Lea, puzzled by his question, could only stare blankly. "I don't understand what you mean."

Darren shook his head, his expression one of pity. "Now that the truth is out in the open, you don't have to pretend to be a vacationing tourist staying in a small room. I see that your company spares no expenses when it comes to creature comforts," he said, glancing around at the elegantly appointed room.

"What do you want?" This time, as she repeated her question, her voice held an edge of anger and reflected none of the anguish in her heart.

"What do I want? I want to know why?" he growled, stepping closer to Lea.

Dear Reader:

Nora Roberts, Tracy Sinclair, Jeanne Stephens, Carole Halston, Linda Howard. Are these authors familiar to you? We hope so, because they are just a few of our most popular authors who publish with Silhouette Special Edition each and every month. And the Special Edition list is changing to include new writers with fresh stories. It has been said that discovering a new author is like making a new friend. So during these next few months, be sure to look for books by Sandi Shane, Dorothy Glenn and other authors who have just written their first and second Special Editions, stories we hope you enjoy.

Choosing which Special Editions to publish each month is a pleasurable task, but not an easy one. We look for stories that are sophisticated, sensuous, touching, and great love stories, as well. These are the elements that make Silhouette Special Editions more romantic . . . and unique.

So we hope you'll find this Silhouette Special Edition just that—*Special*—and that the story finds a special place in your heart.

The Editors at Silhouette

SERL-7/85

MONICA BARRIE
A Perfect Vision

Silhouette Special Edition

Published by Silhouette Books New York

America's Publisher of Contemporary Romance

SILHOUETTE BOOKS
300 E. 42nd St., New York, N.Y. 10017

Copyright © 1985 by Monica Barrie

Distributed by Pocket Books

ISBN: 0-373-09267-9

First Silhouette Books printing October 1985

10 9 8 7 6 5 4 3 2 1

America's Publisher of Contemporary Romance

Printed in the U.S.A.

MONICA BARRIE,

a native of New York State, has traveled extensively around the world but returned to settle in New York. A prolific romance writer, Monica creates tightly woven emotional stories that are drawn from her understanding of relationships between men and women.

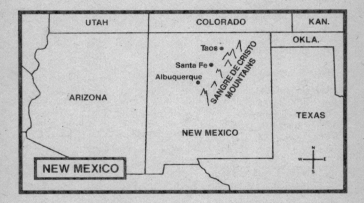

UTAH   COLORADO   KAN.

OKLA.

Taos

Santa Fe
Albuquerque

ARIZONA

SANGRE DE CRISTO
MOUNTAINS

TEXAS

NEW MEXICO

NEW MEXICO

Chapter One

The scent of pine was heavy in the air, rising from the unspoiled valley as Lea Graham walked precariously along its slope. Even with heavy hiking boots, she had to walk carefully on the rock-strewn earth, her eyes focused far below her.

She did not see the manzanita bushes that brushed her calves, nor did she notice the clump of piñon pines to her left. All Lea saw was the smooth floor of the small valley, and what she envisioned for its future.

The sun was moving toward the western peaks of the Sangre de Cristo Mountains, and Lea had been walking along the edge of the valley since noon. Her mind was filled with the potential and the possibilities that had been her dream for so many years, and that, for the past two years, had slowly become a reality.

Lea Graham was an architect; not just an architect, but an environmental designer as well, following in the footsteps of her mother. Janice Graham had been in the forefront of environmental architecture even before the popular hue and cry for ecological controls.

Yet her mother had never been given the proper recognition for the work she'd done. No, Janice Graham had been years ahead of her time. Because she was a woman in a male-dominated profession, Janice Graham had never been acknowledged for her innovative techniques; the men of the architectural firm she worked for had taken all the credit for her designs.

On the other hand, Lea's mother had never seemed to care for acclaim; she had been happy to do what she loved to do—design structures for a realistic American lifestyle. Lea Graham felt the same, except that she would never allow other people to take credit for what she worked so hard to accomplish.

Lea was about to complete her first major project, a project she had been working on, exclusively, for the past two years. The project had become her life, and because of her strong dedication to it, she'd had to sacrifice a great deal. *Too much?* she asked herself.

No! she answered emphatically.

Sighing, Lea looked across the small valley to the far slopes. This was her third and longest trip to New Mexico. With each trip, her anticipation of the next step of the project grew intensely. Her excitement for the project had grown in equal proportion to the time she'd spent working on it.

Lea smiled as she thought of how the fates had guided her that day two years before when she'd discovered her chance to turn her dream into a reality. Even now, she still found it difficult to believe that she was actually accomplishing her goal. It had simply been her good fortune to overhear a conversation that she wasn't supposed to have heard in the first place.

One day at work, Lea was in her office, looking over the figures for a shopping mall, when she discovered she'd left one of the fact sheets in Robert Kanter's office. Robert Kanter was the director of development and her boss. Because it had been after closing time, and she'd thought everyone had gone home, she went to her boss's office and opened the door before she heard voices.

Not meaning to eavesdrop, Lea immediately started to close the door, but the conversation between Kanter and another man caused her to stop in her tracks.

After listening for several minutes, Lea finally closed the door and returned to her office to digest what she'd learned. Her boss had been speaking of a new land development deal outside Santa Fe. What she'd heard had sent her thoughts spinning, for it was the very thing she had always wanted to do.

Without anyone's knowledge, and working at home at night, Lea designed the entire master plan for a new mixed residential community that utilized the environment as part of the design—the very concept she had overheard her boss speaking of.

In a bold and risky step, because no one had actually confirmed the possibility of the New Mexico deal, she went to the director of development with her ideas. Her first step was to confess that she had overheard his talk about the Santa Fe land development. Although he seemed somewhat taken aback about her revelation, he also was impressed enough by what she told him and showed to him, to assign her to begin the first part of the architectural design proposal.

Three months later, Lea went far beyond the first-step proposal, and had shown Kanter a finished proposal, incorporating all her ideas about mixed community living. Kanter seemed duly impressed. But nothing else was said for several months. Then, one day, she was called into Kanter's office, and learned that her proposal had been accepted, and that a cost and feasibility study was going to be made.

"By whom?" Lea asked.

"I don't know as yet," Kanter responded.

"I want to do it. I want to do the entire job."

Kanter shook his head slowly at her request. "Lea, your proposal is good, but you don't have the experience—none of us really does. Designing a special community that utilizes the environment is not something done every day."

"I have more experience than anyone else in the firm," she'd quickly countered. "Or have you forgotten who my mother was?"

"No," Robert had said with a quick shake of his head, "I haven't forgotten."

"You know that this type of project is exactly what you hired me for. What good is an assistant director of development, if not to do the job I'm being paid for?"

"It's not that," Kanter began, but Lea cut him off.

"Oh? Is it because I'm still a novice, or because I'm a woman?" she challenged.

"That's unfair," Kanter had retorted. "If it was because you are a woman, you wouldn't have the job now."

"Then is it because of my lack of hands-on experience?"

"Partly," Kanter admitted.

"I can do it!" Lea declared. "Try me. I've been studying this type of community for years. Please," she'd added in a less provocative tone.

"I can't spare you for this project. We have too many other things going on. You know that this project has to be worked on exclusively."

"I can do it, and handle other things if I have to," Lea argued.

"It could also cost you your job," Kanter stated.

Lea stared at him for several long seconds while his words sank into her mind. Then she realized that Robert Kanter was speaking out of concern for her.

Kanter had hired Lea straight from college, and had supervised her work for the first two years of her employment, helping her, teaching her, and working with her. At the end of her second year, she had taken her licensing exam, and had passed it, thus becoming a registered architect. After she had passed the test, she had also been given a promotion, and had been named Assistant to the Director of Development.

"Please, Robert, I need to do this project."

"Let me think about it," Kanter told her. "And you think about it also. If anything were to go wrong with the project, it could mean your job."

Lea shook her head. "I don't have to think about it. I want to do the project. I need to do it!"

"You don't have to prove yourself to me," Kanter said.

Lea smiled. "I know that, Robert. But perhaps I need to prove something to myself," she admitted honestly.

A week later, Lea was called in to a meeting with Robert Kanter and James Lansing, president of the Lansing and Mitchell Architectural Corporation—the firm Lea worked for.

The meeting had lasted fifteen minutes. At the end, Lea was told that she was in charge of the Santa Fe project. She was given three years to prepare everything. Construction was to begin three years from the date of that meeting. Only one other item was discussed; it was the need to keep every last detail of the project secret. No one was to learn of the project, especially not the residents of Santa Fe. The reasons for this were based on a combination of the fear of price gouging by the contractors and the reaction from environmentalists.

Although those types of problems always plagued a major development, and would normally be accounted for in the cost estimates of the construction, they were problems that could easily interrupt or even destroy a project as large and as sensitive as this one.

The only person outside the firm who would know anything about the project was one man in New Mexico. His name was Randolph Hastings, and he was an independent architect who would be the New Mexican architect of record for the project. Randolph Hastings had worked with Lansing and Mitchell many times in the past. He was also trusted implicitly by the firm, and was considered to be above reproach.

When Lea had left the meeting, she had been walking on a cloud. Her mind had been filled with excitement, and not a little trepidation. That very afternoon she had begun to outline the master plan, and, three weeks later, had flown to Santa Fe to look over the valley that had been chosen for the site.

Lea exhaled slowly, gazing at the overwhelming beauty surrounding her. She had devoted two years to this project, two long, sometimes happy, but predominantly hard, years. Almost all of her waking moments were spent working on the project, and a good deal of her dreams dwelled on the project, too.

A loud cry drew her attention to the sky. High above the valley she saw a large, dark bird circling. She watched the hawk's graceful flight until it disappeared in the distance, and then she looked down at the valley once again.

"I've given you so much," she whispered to the pine trees on the valley floor below. "So much," she repeated.

Her words were true, yet she knew that this project had helped her to understand what it was she really wanted for her life. Because of the project, she had broken her engagement.

No, not because of the project, she told herself. *Because of who I am.* Reaching a tall tree, Lea stopped walking and rested her back against its trunk, her mind continuing to recall fading memories.

Six months before, she had ended her year-long engagement to Richard Corman, a rising young attorney with the United States Justice Department. It had been her total involvement in the Santa Fe project that had made her realize what her fiancé was really like, and what he wanted in a wife. It had also shown her how mistaken she had been in her belief that she was in love with him.

Seeing the beauty that abounded all around her, Lea felt a lessening of the anger directed at herself, due in part to her feelings about Richard Corman. As she watched the shadows of the tall pine trees lengthen under the afternoon sun, she suddenly relived the last time she and Richard had been together.

Lea nervously paced the confines of the living room of her Potomac town house as she waited for Richard's arrival. On the ring finger of her left hand was a two-carat diamond engagement ring. Two teardrop diamond earrings hung from her earlobes and sparkled brilliantly whenever she passed the lamps set at each end of her couch. A single strand of luminescent pearls graced the skin just above her full breasts.

The black, floor-length formal dress she wore showed her five-foot four-inch height to perfection. Her long sable hair was pinned up in a soft twist centering on the crown of her head. But her green-flecked hazel eyes did not blend with the detached formal facade; they were troubled and distant.

Pausing in her random pacing, Lea turned to the mirrored wall across from her, and looked at the stranger she saw reflected in its surface.

Until a year and a half before, she had never been one to wear an abundance of jewelry or makeup, and only on the most important occasions had she worn formal gowns. But in the past year and a half, her simple business-style wardrobe had changed drastically, even as she had changed. And all in the name of love.

Is it really love? she wondered, studying her face in the mirror. *Why else would I allow myself to change?*

When she'd first started dating Richard Corman, she had been attracted to his strong determination and goals. He was a handsome, urbane man who had an air of purpose, and knew where his future lay.

He was so much the opposite of Lea that she had been attracted to him. Now, eighteen months later, she wasn't at all sure that she'd done the right thing.

Lea shook her head and saw the diamond earrings sparkle enticingly. *This is not me; this is the illusion of who he wants me to be.*

For almost a year, Lea had done her best to make the relationship between her and Richard work, but the harder she tried, the less he worked at it. When she wanted emotion, he showered her with gifts. When she talked of career, he spoke of children and a large house in the Maryland suburbs.

It had taken their engagement to show Lea the type of man that Richard Corman really was. While they had dated, and the romance was still fresh, he had seemed to listen to everything she said, and to agree with her, or at least accept all her views. After they'd become engaged, his attitude toward her had changed drastically.

Lea knew she was expected to dress a certain way, and not only to attend, but to enjoy, all the social functions at which Richard was required to appear. Because he was a rising lawyer in the Justice Department, and the wealthy son of a former U.S. Supreme Court justice,

Richard's life was Washington and politics. Lea soon learned that he expected her life to be the same.

But after following in Richard's footsteps, smiling when she didn't want to and being cheerful and nice when she really wanted to scream and shout, Lea didn't think she could handle any more of it.

"Where is he?" she asked herself as she looked at the gold Cartier watch that Richard had given her two weeks before on her twenty-sixth birthday. In answer to her question, the doorbell rang. Lea opened the door to find Richard wearing a black tuxedo and smiling at her.

"Ready?" he asked without stepping inside.

Lea stared at him and thought she was seeing a stranger. Automatically, she started to nod, but stopped herself. "No!"

"What's wrong?" Richard asked.

"We have to talk."

"Talk?" he asked as he looked at his Rolex. "We'll be late."

"Then we'll be late. Richard, it's only a concert."

"It's more than a concert. We've been invited by the attorney general himself," Richard reminded her in a slightly condescending tone.

"I don't care if we were invited by the president!" she snapped.

"Lea," he said in a soft voice as he slowly shook his head.

"Come inside, Richard, we need to talk."

Richard looked at his watch again. "Lea—"

"No. Come inside."

Richard shrugged his shoulders and entered the small town house. After Lea closed the door, she led him into the living room. Then, while she stared at him, she slowly shook her head. "It won't work."

"What won't work?" he asked.

"Us. We won't work."

"I don't understand. Why won't we work? We love each other, don't we?"

"Do we?" Angrily, Lea shook her head. "I love you, Richard, at least I thought I did. But lately I'm not so sure."

"Don't I give you enough?" Richard asked suddenly, his gaze shifting to the earrings, and then to the pearl necklace.

"No, you don't!" Before he could respond, Lea held out both hands defensively before her. "You give me wonderful gifts, Richard. But jewelry and furs are just things. I need more than things, Richard. I need emotional support and love. Incidentally, love isn't something you buy."

"Are you saying I'm trying to buy you?" he asked, his voice growing tense as he stared at her.

"No," Lea whispered. "What I'm saying is that your idea of love is different from mine. I don't want the gifts you buy for me. Richard, I want your love, not your money. I don't want to spend my life being a fashion-plate, living in a mansion filled with servants and doing nothing except shopping and wasting my life."

"There are worse things," he said, his voice again condescending.

"Yes, there are," Lea admitted. "But that's relative to each person."

"What's wrong with living in a large house and raising a family with the security I can provide?"

Gazing at Richard, Lea saw that his question was sincerely put. "Nothing. But it's not what I want. I have my career, Richard, and that is part of my life."

"But when we're married, you won't have to work."

"I don't work because I *have* to; I work because I *want* to. I love my work!"

"More than me, it seems."

His words struck her painfully, and accented the differences between them that he couldn't recognize. "No, Richard, but you never could see that. Since the day we became engaged, my life has meant nothing to you. I became an adornment, a social asset to be used for your career. And what will happen after we marry? Will I become a brood mare for your blue-blooded children?"

Lea knew that she shouldn't allow her anger to surface, but could not help it; her calm words were having absolutely no effect on him. "That is what you want from a wife, isn't it? Children and a social hostess. Perhaps I could do a little volunteer work at the hospital also?"

"Lea!" Richard snapped, his temper flaring for the first time, but Lea wouldn't let him continue; she knew he would talk about his mother, and that volunteer work and raising a family had been her highest priority after her husband.

"Don't misunderstand me, Richard. There is nothing wrong with having a family or doing volunteer work. I'm just not ready to do that yet. I have other things I need to accomplish."

"Have I ever interfered with your work?" he asked.

"Ignoring it can be just as bad as interference. At least be honest, Richard! You've never been interested in what I do. All you care about is your career. Not once in the past year have you ever asked about my work. When I talk about the project I'm involved with, you always find a way to change the subject. I attend all your social events without question, but you never have the time to go to mine. I've accepted this situation for as long as I could. I tried to believe that you loved me, and I loved you, but I can't accept it any more.''

"Is that what you care about? Making it big as an architect?" Richard shook his head sadly. "Or are you trying to live up to the image you've created of your mother? Are you trying to prove to the world that Janice Graham's daughter is as great as her mother?"

The cruelty of his words had a biting, angered twist to them that hurt Lea more than anything else he might have said at that moment. He had used her respect and admiration for her mother's accomplishments against her, and not one word of what he had said was the truth. "That was uncalled for," she whispered.

"Was it? Or is it the truth? Is your career more important than anything else, Lea?"

"No, Richard, it's not more important," she said in a suddenly calm voice. "But it's just as important as anything else. I'm sorry, Richard," Lea whispered as she slipped the engagement ring from her finger and extended it toward him.

"You're making a big mistake," Richard warned, his voice suddenly cold.

As he spoke, Lea heard no real emotion behind his words, no sadness or sorrow. Intuitively, she realized that what he was feeling was disappointment that he would have to start over again and find another woman who he thought would be pretty enough to become his wife.

"In your eyes I probably am making a mistake," Lea said. "But I know better. Please leave."

After the door clicked close, Lea stared at it. "So much for love," she whispered, unable to hold back her tears. Even though she had been prepared for what had happened, she had secretly hoped that Richard would understand what she'd said, and that he would listen to her and perhaps accept what she wanted.

She had hoped that they might find a way to compromise, and to renew the love she had thought she'd once had for him. But tonight had proven one thing to Lea. She had learned that her idea of love, and Richard's, were too different to ever keep them together.

"No, Richard," she said aloud. "I didn't make the mistake, you did." Then she took off the diamond earrings, the pearl necklace, and the Cartier watch. She went upstairs to her bedroom, where she collected all the expensive gifts he had showered upon her over the past year, and put them all in a box. She would return everything he had given her. Everything!

"Fool," Lea whispered to herself as she tried to pull her thoughts out of the past. Even after she'd returned all of Richard's gifts, she had kept the hope alive that he would come to his senses and remember the love he had always said he felt for her. Never once could she admit to herself that it might have been her pride that made her feel that way, and not what she had once considered to be love.

But he hadn't returned to her. In fact, he never once called or wrote. Two months after she had broken their engagement, she attended a political dinner with her boss, Robert Kanter, and his wife, and saw Richard sitting across the room with a strikingly beautiful woman, whose plastic smile seemed to have been sculpted onto her face. In that moment, Lea had breathed a sigh of relief, knowing that she had done exactly the right thing in breaking her engagement and freeing herself to start once again on the road to becoming her own person, and not someone else's adornment.

Smiling to herself, Lea drew away from the tree she had been leaning on, and looked again at the beautiful slopes that led down into the valley.

It will be lovely, she told herself, thinking of the way the valley would be transformed from earth, rock, and trees into a viable community that would house four hundred families.

Looking around, Lea spotted an outcrop of boulders at the edge of a steep slope. Her legs were tiring from the two hours of hiking, and the tan-and-gray rock structure looked inviting and comfortable.

She went to the outcrop of rocks and picked one that was somewhat level to sit on. Sighing as the weight was taken from her feet, Lea again looked down into the valley. From where she sat, the downward angle appeared more dramatic, and she was suddenly aware of how much steeper this slope seemed in comparison to the view from the valley floor. While she was studying the land that would soon be transformed into a useful community, she heard a movement behind her.

Turning quickly, she found herself staring into the red mouth of a huge lizard. Time seemed to come to a halt as a cold chill of fear gripped her. She clearly saw the flicking tongue darting from its mouth and saw, too, a band of dark stripes around its neck.

She moved quickly, propelling herself away from it. When her feet landed on the earth, she lost her footing, fell to the ground, and began to roll. A second later, she realized that she was near the brink of the rocky ledge, and about to slide past it.

Fear made her muscles stronger. Frantically, she searched for a handhold. Her hands scraped the ground, her fingers curled into grasping claws. Suddenly, she caught the edge of a deeply embedded rock with one hand. She felt one fingernail break, and then felt the pain in one arm as her body jerked to a stop. With her eyes shut tightly, Lea held on and stopped her downward plunge.

The pain in her hand, arm, and shoulder was like a screaming nightmare. *Fight!* she ordered herself. She raised her other hand and grabbed the rock, taking pressure off her left shoulder. Slowly, she tried to pull herself up.

She felt the rock shift. Exhaling sharply, Lea froze. Her eyes were still closed. She knew better than to look down. *Pull!* she commanded herself. Again, she began to draw her body up, and again, the rock threatened to give way.

She started to panic as pain flared up in her shoulders. Her fingers were slipping and she frantically tried to find a new purchase.

"Don't move!" came a husky, deep voice. An instant later a strong hand gripped her wrist and began to pull her up.

Lea felt the rocky earth scrape her chest, stomach, and thighs, but she didn't care. The pain in her shoulders became more intense; but that, too, was unimportant. Someone had found her and was helping her. That was important.

A moment later her wrist was released, and she felt the same strong hands slip under her arms and help lift her onto her feet. Only then did she open her eyes.

"Are you all right?" asked her savior.

As had happened moments before, time again stood still as Lea's eyes locked onto the endlessly deep blue-gray eyes of the man who had saved her. Looking up into his face, she was suddenly aware of how handsome the man was, and how his short dark beard did not hide his well-chiseled features. Although the pain in her arms was already subsiding, she knew it wasn't fear that held her voice a prisoner; it was this sudden apparition.

Chapter Two

I...I'm fine," Lea finally managed to say, her mind still dizzy from her narrow escape.

"If you're going to walk in this area, you should at least look around you occasionally," he commented, his white teeth flashing brightly in contrast to the darkness of his beard.

Blinking her eyes several times, Lea tried to make herself relax. Despite her efforts, her heart still pumped furiously. "I...I didn't think it was dangerous to walk around here. That lizard—" she began, turning to point at the rocks she'd been sitting on.

"That lizard is harmless. It's not something to be afraid of."

"It startled me," Lea said defensively.

"Are you usually so easily startled?" he asked.

"No," Lea replied. "Thank you for coming to my rescue," she added.

"I was doing it as much for myself as for you," he stated. "If you had fallen, this place would be swarming with people. A helicopter would have had to come to lift you out of the valley and take you to a hospital. Reporters and curious tourists would trample all over the area and I wouldn't be able to work for days."

The stranger's rude speech was like a slap, and Lea's anger surged. She forced a modicum of control on herself, knowing that no matter what he'd said, he had saved her. Sighing, she stretched out her arm and offered him her hand.

"Well, thank you anyway for helping me out. I'm Lea Graham," she added as she glanced down at the hand he offered to her. In the instant before his hand grasped hers, she saw that his fingers were stained with assorted shades of oil paints.

"Darren Laird," he said, taking her hand in a firm grip. "And, you're welcome."

Strangely, while his hand held hers, Lea felt a warmth emanate from him. She stared at him while the heat turned into slow fire, until, mercifully, he released her hand. But even when he was no longer touching her, she could feel lingering traces of his fingers on her skin.

"What are you doing up here alone?" he asked, his eyes fixed on hers.

"Looking around," she replied noncommittally. "And you?"

"As I said before, I'm working." In accent to his statement, Darren pointed toward a level spot a hundred feet from where they stood.

Turning slightly, she followed the direction he was pointing in, and saw an easel set up next to a tree. It was positioned at such an angle that she could not possibly have seen it while walking near the cliff.

"Work?" she asked. "You're a painter?"

"I've been called worse."

The way he said it made Lea pause. Glancing quickly back at the easel, Lea shrugged her shoulders. "An artist, I mean."

With that, Darren took Lea's elbow, guiding her away from the rocks and toward the spot where his easel stood. As they walked, she rubbed absently at the pain in her shoulders. When they reached the easel, Lea halted abruptly, her breath catching.

"It's magnificent," she whispered, looking at the landscape that he was painting. She saw the rocks she had been sitting on moments ago, and even recognized the sketchy outline of the collared lizard perching on a rock.

"Are you staying nearby?" Darren asked.

"Is it that obvious that I'm not from around here?" Lea asked, without taking her eyes from the canvas.

"To me, yes."

Lea shifted her gaze from the canvas to the man. "In Santa Fe. At La Fonda."

Darren nodded thoughtfully, his eyes locked on Lea's. "You know, when someone rescues another, it's customary to offer a reward."

Lea was shocked by his unexpected statement. Several moments passed before she could speak. "Why...I...of course," she finally said. Colored by her temper, her question was laced with sarcasm. "How much do you charge for playing the white knight?"

Darren Laird's laughter was soft in her ears; the amused twinkle in his blue-gray eyes sent a chill up her spine. "Dinner is my fee. I'll pick you up at eight."

Her anger faded and her stomach tightened. A moment later her tongue flicked out to moisten her lips. "All right," she whispered.

Standing before the mirror, Lea adjusted the neckline of her dress. Although the forest green material fell smoothly, she was far from satisfied with the way it looked.

After rearranging it pointlessly one more time, she gave up, admitting that it was her nerves and not the dress that was at fault.

She stared at the filed-down broken fingernail on her left hand and could almost feel the scraping of rock against her skin, along with the powerful grip of Darren Laird's hand on her wrist. Ever since she'd driven away from the small valley, she'd been unable to get Darren out of her thoughts. Each time she relaxed her guard, she would feel his hand holding hers, and feel, too, the heat that had flared so unexpectedly at his touch.

Why did I agree to have dinner with him? she wondered. She hadn't accepted a date from anyone since breaking her engagement to Richard. She was especially wary of the seemingly overconfident artist who had appeared so suddenly in her life.

He's too handsome, she told herself. Yet she sensed that Darren's good looks were something the man himself was unaware of; she had seen that when they'd talked earlier. Lea shivered involuntarily as Darren's image grew before her. He was six feet tall, with wide shoulders, a trim waist, and long legs.

She had never been attracted to men with beards, but she couldn't imagine Darren's face without the short cropped border of dark hair. It accented his sensuous mouth, sparkling white teeth, and intense eyes. When he'd smiled at her, the pattern of crow's-feet that radiated from the corners of his eyes had caused her heart to beat wildly.

Stop! she commanded herself as she pressed her hands together. But she could no more stop her wildly cascading thoughts than she could control her anxiety. From the first moment she'd looked into her rescuer's face, the fear of her narrow escape from injury—or worse—had been wiped from her mind, replaced by a sudden and unexpected attraction to the handsome stranger. Closing her eyes, Lea reminded herself that she had no time to become involved with a man; she was too involved with her work.

As she opened her eyes and turned to look at the small travel clock she'd brought with her, the phone rang. Her stomach twisted; her mouth went dry. Slowly, she went to the phone and picked it up. "Hello."

"Hello, Lea, I'm in the lobby."

"I'll be right there," she said. After hanging up, she took a deep breath. *That was easy,* she said silently.

Five minutes later she strode across La Fonda's lobby, directly toward Darren. She took in his appearance, almost nodding in approval at the way he looked in his simple yet superbly tailored blue suit. A pale gray shirt and burgundy tie completed the picture. Her eyes flicked to his feet, and she noted that he wore black western boots. When she looked at his face again, she saw him smile.

"Do I pass?" he asked when she stopped two feet in front of him.

"Pass?"

"Inspection."

Lea blushed, trying her best to ignore it. "You look very nice," she said, complimenting him instead of making an excuse.

"Thank you. That particular shade of green works well with your skin tones," he said matter-of-factly.

"Coming from an artist, I guess I can take that as a compliment," she replied.

"No, it's the truth."

Again Lea blushed; this time she could not ignore it. "Thank you," she whispered. "Do you always speak so—ah...candidly?"

"Why not? Are you hungry?" Darren asked.

"I don't know," Lea replied honestly.

"Shall we find out?" he asked, offering her his arm.

"Yes," Lea said, as she placed her hand on his arm.

They walked out the hotel door and stepped into the cool night. "Are we walking or driving?"

"Walking, if you don't mind. The restaurant is only a few blocks from here."

"That's fine. I like walking at night," she added, favoring Darren with a smile.

They fell into a comfortable silence while they walked along the street. Three blocks from the hotel, Darren turned and guided her into the restaurant.

The restaurant's Southwestern decor was warm and appealing. The hangings on the wood tongue-and-groove wall paneling reflected an Indian influence, and the paintings were a combination of Western land-scapes and Mexican scenes. The highly polished wood tables were spaced comfortably apart, and the lighting was bright enough to see by but low enough to lend an air of privacy.

After being seated and ordering cocktails, Darren gazed at Lea, taking in the soft lines of her face. He noticed that she wore a minimum of makeup, and found himself approving of the way she had applied it. While he saw the telltale lines of tension at the corners of her mouth, he knew that time would help to relax her. But even the slight tightness of her features did not lessen the impact of her beauty.

"And do I?" Lea asked suddenly.

"What?" Darren replied, his expression puzzled.

"Pass inspection?" she finished with a smile.

"Absolutely!"

"Is that the artist talking, or the man?" she joked, embarrassed by his forthright reply.

"They are one and the same," Darren stated. Watching her, he sensed her discomfort. "Lea, you're a beautiful woman. Why does that embarrass you?"

Lea shrugged her shoulders, but did not take her eyes from Darren's. "I—"

"Don't misunderstand me," Darren added, his face calm, his voice low. "As an artist I look at things differently than most. When I see beauty, I either paint it or compliment it. Sometimes I do both. It's my way.''

"Thank you," Lea said at last. The cocktails arrived just in time to save her from wondering what would happen next.

Lifting their glasses, they toasted each other silently, in the way that newly acquainted people do, speaking not with words, but with gestures. After taking a sip, Lea put her drink down. "This seems a pleasant restaurant," she commented.

"It is," Darren replied. "How long will you be in Santa Fe?"

"Another few weeks," she answered noncommittally.

"Good. Then where do you go?"

Lea smiled. "Home. I live in Potomac, Maryland, just outside of Washington, D.C."

"I've been there. It's quite pleasant for an urban area."

"Yes, it is, though I never thought of it in those terms."

"Are you hungry yet?" Darren asked.

"As a matter of fact, yes," Lea said. Picking up the menu, she opened it and glanced at the offerings.

"Everything is good," Darren told her.

Looking at the menu gave Lea a chance to clear her mind. She knew that Darren's questions were only meant as innocent conversation designed to help them get acquainted, but she had found herself becoming guarded. She was certain that Darren was just who he said he was, but the development project was something she must not speak of. So far she had not said anything about work. She hoped it would stay that way.

"The mountain trout is excellent," Darren suggested while he watched her look over the menu. After he spoke, she closed the menu and smiled at him.

"Then trout it shall be."

A moment later the waitress appeared and took their order. When she left, Lea looked at Darren. "Tell me about yourself, Darren Laird."

Darren gazed intently at her, his eyes unmoving, his mouth held in a straight line. "I'm thirty-three years old; I'm a painter; and I've never rescued anyone before."

Silence fell. Obviously, he had no intention of telling her anything else, especially anything personal.

"I thought that only cowboys were the strong silent type," Lea said, a smile easing the tension on her face.

Darren shrugged his shoulders. "You asked me to tell you about myself. I did."

"Your verbosity isn't exactly overwhelming."

Darren lifted his hands and looked at them for several seconds before speaking. "I use another medium to communicate," he stated.

Lea studied his long, graceful, strong fingers which still had specks of paint on them. Then she drew her gaze from his hands, to stare deeply into his eyes. "Why, Darren? Why are we here, together?"

"Because we want to be," Darren answered. Then he smiled.

Lea's heart was racing again, and her mouth became parched. Tension hung so thickly in the air around them that she thought she would suffocate. Forcing herself to break the bonds of the trance-like moment, she blinked several times and lifted her glass.

After taking a sip, she sighed. "If you won't tell me about yourself, at least tell me about your work. Do you paint anything besides landscapes?"

Darren nodded slowly. "I paint those things which I feel a need to paint. But usually I don't choose my subjects, they choose me."

"Did the valley we were at today choose you?"

"It chose me a long time ago," Darren said. Then, after taking a deep breath, he began to talk about the valley, and the wildlife that he loved to paint.

The combination of Darren's voice and the excellent dinner worked a magical spell on Lea. By the time coffee was served, Lea was relaxed.

"And now you know all about me," Darren said, his face suddenly stoic.

"All about you—no. A little about your work, perhaps."

"My work is my life," he said in a low voice.

Lea shook her head slowly. "I doubt that."

Darren's eyes flickered, his mouth tensed. "Do you? Why?"

"You're not that uncomplicated," she told him, her eyes sweeping across his face, her pulse becoming erratic as she took in the handsome visage before her. "There's much more to you than being an artist."

"Perhaps."

Lea watched him and saw, with his single word, a curtain drop across his eyes. Intuitively, she knew that the time to probe was over, for now.

Then Darren smiled, and the tension that filled the air lessened. "I am very glad I was at the valley today," he stated.

Lea shivered as she vividly remembered her near-disaster. "So am I," she said fervently.

"If I hadn't been there," he added in a low, husky voice that sent a chill racing along her spine, "I wouldn't have met you, and we wouldn't be having dinner together."

Lea smiled. "If you hadn't been there, I wouldn't be having dinner with anyone right now...except for a lizard or two."

"Touché," Darren said with a smile that matched her own. But a second later, his face became serious. "Do you believe in fate, Lea?"

Lea's breath caught; her pulse pounded in her neck and her gaze could not leave his face. When she spoke, it was in a barely audible voice. "I believe in making my own decisions, of picking the paths I walk and being in control of my life."

Darren nodded, his eyes again changing, taking on a distant and thoughtful cast for a moment. "Perhaps fate means only that we were both drawn to the same place at the same time, not that anything else was to happen."

"I..." Lea stopped, knowing that she couldn't tell him it was not fate but her own work that had brought her to the valley at this particular time. Instead of finishing her reply, she shrugged her shoulders uncomfortably.

Then Darren shook his head. "Tell me why you picked Santa Fe for a vacation?"

The tension holding Lea in its grip grew tighter while she tried to form her answer. The lie that rested on the tip of her tongue tasted bitter, but once again she knew she could not speak the truth—not yet, not until she knew him better.

"Why not? It's lovely, clean, and the air is breatheable."

Darren nodded at her words. "That it is. And what do you do when you're not on vacation?" he asked.

"Just work," she said simply.

"No," Darren stated, "I don't think you do 'just' anything. I sense passions in you. Passions that guide you."

Lea smiled weakly, suddenly embarrassed by the depth of his insight. "I'm an architect."

"Then you're an artist too."

Lea shook her head. "A designer perhaps, not an artist."

"Look up the definition of an artist. It doesn't just imply painting or sculpting. Do you like your work?"

Lea smiled. "I love my work."

"I thought so. It makes the difference between being good and being great. I don't think anything you could do would be just good."

Again, Lea felt the heat of a blush. But this time it was caused by a spark of anger at his overconfident remarks. "How can you say that when you don't know me?"

Darren didn't smile. Slowly and deliberately, he lifted his hand and reached across the table to cover hers. His eyes never wavered from her face; his voice was husky and deep. "I know you better than you think. You're a special person, Lea Graham."

The warmth from his hand penetrated her skin. Her stomach tightened, her heart fluttered. She tried to speak, but could not. All she could do was stare at him. "We just met," she whispered at last.

"I know," Darren replied when he lifted his hand from hers. "Remind me to thank that lizard."

Lea laughed despite her unease. She was able to relax even more. "For a minute I thought you were being serious."

Darren's eyes narrowed slightly. "You know I was." Then he turned to signal the waitress. While he paid the check, Lea gathered her wits about her.

Everything he had said, and the way he'd said it, had left her no doubts as to her own feelings. She was very attracted to Darren Laird. More attracted to him than she wanted to admit. At the same time, she felt guilty for having lied to him about being in Santa Fe on vacation. Even so, she'd had no choice in that. She knew that no word must ever get out about the valley project until the time was right.

"Ready?" Darren asked after the waitress had left.

"For?—" she asked immediately, suddenly not wanting the evening to end.

"A place I know."

"What kind of a place?" she asked guardedly.

Darren shook his head sadly. "I save you from possible death, certain injury at the least, not to mention a very bouncy ride down the side of a mountain—"

"—hill."

"In these parts, hills are only bumps on mountains. Trust me, Lea."

Lea raised her eyebrows at him. "I've heard those words before."

"Never from me," Darren stated in a deep, meaningful tone.

A moment later, Lea nodded her head. "Lead on, white knight."

"Thank you, fair damsel."

When they left the restaurant, Darren guided them toward the plaza, but before they reached it, he turned onto another narrow side street. After passing adobe buildings, he escorted her into a small club, where soft, romantic music filled the dimly lit interior. On the dance floor, couples danced slowly near the three-piece band, and the low hum of conversation could be heard above the music.

As they walked toward a vacant table, Lea noticed how often people said hello to Darren, and how their eyes were frankly curious when they strayed to her. Once they were seated, Lea let out a low sigh. "You're a popular man," she said.

"I was born near here. I've known most of these people all my life."

"They sure are wondering who I am."

"Yes, aren't they?" he stated with a slow smile. "Drink?"

"Club soda, if I may."

"You may," Darren stated, just as a waitress approached the table. He ordered a club soda with lime for Lea, and brandy for himself.

Before the drinks arrived, Darren stood. "Dance?"

Lea, suddenly unable to speak, stood and let him lead her onto the dance floor. Even before his arm went around her to draw her close, she was leaning toward him. When his hand settled on the small of her back, a low sigh escaped her lips.

Stop, she tried to tell herself. But it felt good to be held by Darren, good and secure. She smelled the subtle masculine scent that clung to his skin, part aftershave, part Darren. She liked it.

His hand held hers tightly as they moved to the music. Their eyes stayed locked on each other's, and she found herself following his graceful movements wherever he led.

The heat of his body against hers was a constant reminder of how close she was to him; she could feel the way the muscles in his chest moved, even through their clothing. Gentle flames spread from where his hand rested at the small of her back. Confusion, tension, anxiety, and anticipation all combined to make her dizzy.

By the time the dance ended, Lea thought she would faint. Never before had she reacted so strongly to a dance. *To a man,* she corrected herself sternly.

"You dance beautifully," she told Darren.

"Thank you, but I rarely dance."

"Rarely or not, it was lovely."

Silence descended, and neither Darren nor Lea seemed to mind. Lea felt as though she were in another world, and had left the real world behind. They listened to the music, talked about nothing in particular, and danced whenever the mood hit them. Only when the lights in the club were flicked on and off did Lea realize that the hours had flown by and the night was over.

Ten minutes later, Lea was standing outside the door to her room. Darren took her key and opened the door. Then he turned to her, and the smile was gone from his face. "Lea, I want to thank—"

Lea's hand flew to his mouth, stopping him in mid-sentence. "No. Thank you, Darren," she whispered, taking her hand from his lips.

Before her arm fell to her side, Darren reached out and drew her to him. Her eyes were opened wide as his head descended; they closed only when her arms went around him, and their lips came together.

The kiss was like an explosion. Lea's heart and mind burst the instant their lips met. Flames roared within her, and a desire was born that she'd never before thought possible.

The kiss lasted for a long time and, when their mouths finally parted, Lea's breathing was ragged. This was a new weakness she had discovered within herself. "Darren—"

Darren would not let her speak. "I want to see you again. Tomorrow, all right?"

Lea stared at him. The unexpectedness of his request, and the lingering aftereffects of the all-consuming kiss, kept her tongue still. But her eyes, sweeping everywhere over his face, gave him the answer.

"I'll be by in the morning to take you sight-seeing," he told her in a low but steady voice.

Rather than try to speak, Lea nodded.

Then he bent and brushed his lips across hers quickly. An instant later, he walked away.

Lea watched him until he disappeared, and only then did she enter her room and close the door. Leaning her back against the door, she closed her eyes. "What's happening to me?" she asked aloud.

An hour later, Lea was lying in bed, wide awake. She had tried to make herself fall asleep, but failed. Troubling thoughts paraded madly through her head, thoughts of that afternoon, and of the evening just ended.

Whenever she closed her eyes, Darren's face would appear on the backs of her lids. His strong features, the dark border of his beard, and his shining eyes conspired to keep her from sleeping.

Opening her eyes suddenly, Lea sat up. With a quick flick of her outstretched hand, she turned on the bedside lamp. *Not now! This is the wrong time to get involved!* she told herself. Although she tried to be firm with herself, she soon realized the futility of her efforts.

During dinner, and then throughout the rest of the evening, as they had danced and talked, Lea had found herself growing more and more attracted to Darren. It was a realization that had slowly worked its way into her consciousness, and one that now scared her more than she wanted to admit.

Lea had just ended one relationship that had almost cost her her identity. Although she had attributed her lack of dating to her heavy work schedule, she knew that the real reason was a fear of entanglement in another complicated relationship that would hold her back from her career goals.

Darren was the first man she had gone out with since Richard, the first man she had even wanted to share her time with. But she knew she could not allow anything to develop between them.

The memory of their deep and passionate kiss over-shadowed her thoughts, and Lea felt her body again responding to the need and desires that Darren's lips had brought so quickly to the surface. "No," she whispered. "I can't let this happen."

Then why did I agree to see him tomorrow? she asked herself.

Lea exhaled sharply and made herself think about anything except Darren Laird. In her mind she painted a picture of the small valley, and imagined the completion of her project. She envisioned the four hundred families living and working within the boundaries of the valley, and let the feeling of hope and accomplishment ease tension.

But the instant she lowered her guard again, Darren Laird's handsome face and sensuous lips appeared before her.

"Go away," she whispered to the ethereal vision, but she knew that she could not chase away the image.

Shivering, Lea wrapped her arms around herself protectively. No man had ever affected her the way Darren Laird did. She was deeply taken with him, overwhelmed by the intuition that told her he felt the same toward her.

Will that change when he finds out why I'm really in Santa Fe? she wondered, remembering the way he had described the valley, and the reasons he painted it so often.

Again Lea shivered from the tumult of her thoughts. *Do I want anything more to happen between us?* she wondered. A trace of fear rose within her mind at the thought of entering another relationship.

She shook her head forcefully. *Why am I even thinking about something like that?* But as hard as she tried to forget about Darren, she could not. Something had indeed happened to her this day, and Darren Laird was that something.

Finally, Lea shut off the light, lay back down in the bed, and did her best to ignore her turbulent emotions as she tried to find escape in slumber.

Chapter Three

Sitting in the redwood chair on the deck of his house, Darren watched the sun's slow ascent into the sky. The night had been long and filled with thought and introspection, introspection of his life, and thoughts of Lea Graham.

After returning home the night before, he had undressed and tried to sleep, but had found sleep elusive. A restless hour and a half passed before Darren had left the bed, put on jeans and a shirt, and gone to his studio. There, he'd forced his mind to stop its churning, and went to work on the canvas he'd been painting for the past week.

But as he'd worked, his mind had been plagued with thoughts of Lea and, before he realized what he was doing, he'd found his hands had been working inde-

pendently of his mind. The result had been the start of
a superimposed image of Lea's face over the valley.

Stepping back from the canvas, Darren had stared at
it for endless moments. His earlier remark to Lea, when
they'd been having dinner, returned to haunt him. "I
don't choose my subjects, they choose me." Darren was
never more conscious of the truth of those words.

Slowly, he'd returned to the canvas and begun to
paint again. Four hours later, he'd put his brushes
down, carefully draped a cloth over the canvas, and left
his studio. Sleep had still been the furthest thing from
his mind, and instead of going into the house, he'd gone
out onto the cedar deck, where he'd sat and waited for
the coming of day.

When the first golden edge of the sun rose from behind a mountain peak, Darren sighed with the beauty
it unveiled, a beauty that made him think of Lea, and
his uncharacteristically strong reactions to the woman.

He thought of how he had watched her that afternoon while she walked along the rim of the valley. The
artist in him had been fascinated by the lone silhouette
that contrasted so starkly with the trees and mountains, and had been thankful that she had not noticed
him sitting near the tall pine tree.

Her long sable hair had shone luxuriously in the sun.
Her slim jeans and blouse had allowed him to see her
true figure. When she had gotten close enough for him
to see her face clearly, he had been surprised at her
beauty. She had smooth, well-defined cheekbones, a
generous mouth, and a small, sloping nose that com-
plemented the rest of her features. Her fair complexion
was a gentle counterpoint to her dark hair.

He had watched her walking, and had seen that she was too preoccupied with her own thoughts to notice him. When she sat on the rocky outcrop, just above the steepest slope of the hill, he had wondered if she knew how near to the edge she was.

. He had seen her startled reaction to the harmless lizard, and watched her jump away from it, only to lose her footing and begin to slide down the side of the hill.

He'd galvanized his body into instant action, running as fast as he could. At the edge of the incline, he had seen her holding on to a small rock. Moving quickly, he'd grabbed her wrists and pulled her up.

What he had not been prepared for was the close-up beauty that made his earlier observations seem pale in comparison. She was not just pretty, she was beautiful. In that instant, when their eyes had met, and their breathing had been louder than any other sound in the valley, Darren had known that he wanted Lea Graham as he had never wanted another woman.

Gazing at the proud golden ball of the early-morning sun, Darren's thoughts continued to play back the previous day's events. When he'd shaken her hand, he had sensed an inner strength, a strength he liked immediately. He had admired her ability to recover quickly, along with the sense of humor she'd displayed even while frightened. *Yes,* he thought, *Lea Graham is quite a lady. But not for me!*

Darren closed his eyes as he fought against the conflicts that colored his feelings for her. From the moment he'd seen her, he had wanted her. But Darren had spent the past four years avoiding social contact as much as possible. He was not sure that he wanted to start again, despite the rush of his newfound emotions for Lea.

Darren had devoted his life to his art and to his passion for keeping the wild and untamed lands free from people who wanted to exploit and develop them. While his art had always been a part of him, the preservation of the land was something that had been growing stronger as the result of another's exploitation of him and his art.

Although he didn't want to think of the past, he couldn't stop the memories. He knew that it was meeting Lea Graham, and having his strongly restrained desires set free, that had once again brought forth the painful reminders.

Darren had spent all his formative years immersed in art. As a young man, he'd been driven to paint. Anything and everything that was set before him had been subject to his artistic interpretations. As he'd worked and developed his craft, he'd learned that nature was his favorite model.

Because of his inner compulsion to paint, he had never developed a large social circle; he had a few close friends and few acquaintances.

Although he had dated during school, he had never had time to give to a relationship. His art had always been the most important thing to him, and now he realized how stunted his social growth had been. With hindsight, it was easy for Darren to look back and place the blame for what had happened on his own naïveté, but back then it hadn't been easy at all.

Darren had never been involved in sports in school, although his body was well muscled and lean. He'd had several affairs, but none had ever evoked any great passions. Only his art had seemed to reach into his heart and his soul.

After studying art at the University of New Mexico, Darren had spent the following two years studying in Paris. When he'd returned home to New Mexico, he'd realized that what he needed to paint had always been surrounding him: the mountains and hills, the trees and bushes, and the animals and people of the Southwest.

Darren had lived a somewhat solitary existence, painting whatever took his fancy, and not caring if he ever sold a work. When he'd had his first large showing in a gallery in Santa Fe, he'd been surprised by the response. Every painting had been sold. It was the first time that Darren had realized how much other people appreciated what he saw and painted.

He had loved the reaction of the people who had bought his paintings, and had continued to paint what he painted best. But six years ago, his life had changed when he'd received a letter from Rebecca Charlow, the owner of the famed Charlow Gallery in New York. She had requested a meeting to discuss, and arrange for, another showing of his work.

A week later, Rebecca Charlow had called, and Darren had found himself agreeing to the show. Ten days after that, Rebecca Charlow had arrived in Santa Fe, at his very doorstep.

Darren had been entranced by the stylish whirlwind from New York City, with her designer clothing, her fashionable hairstyle, and her knowledgeable manner. Two hours after she'd arrived, Darren had promised her that he would have fifteen paintings ready for the show.

Then they'd gone out to dinner. By the time the night had ended, they had become lovers.

Without knowing it at the time, Darren's innocence about women had played him directly into Rebecca Charlow's hands. He had let his emotions run unchecked, like a teenage boy who has discovered passion for the first time. Rebecca Charlow was like no other woman Darren had ever known, and she had bewitched him before he'd become aware of the fact.

Their affair had brought out the physical passions that he'd been unaware he possessed. Because of Rebecca's vast knowledge of the art world, combined with the way she had continually praised his art, Darren had ended up moving east to New York to live with her, and work in a small rented studio in lower Manhattan.

For the following two years, while Rebecca Charlow sold his paintings for higher and higher sums, his work had begun to change without his fully realizing what was happening. When he belatedly discovered the vast changes in himself and his work, it had almost been too late.

Darren's sprawling, powerful scenes of the Southwest's majesty had metamorphosed into the dark visions of a city dweller. While the critics called it his "inner-vision phase," heaping kudos upon him and his work, Rebecca had had no problems obtaining her absurdly high prices.

Finally, after two years, Darren had begun to see past the desires that had been driving him forward. He became aware of how his art had changed, and discovered that he did not like what he saw on the canvases. At the same time, Darren had realized who had truly engineered the transformation of his art. When he told Rebecca of his feelings, she'd dismissed them offhandedly.

"Darren, darling, you're doing so well. You're rich now, and becoming famous. Ninety percent of the artists in New York are mad with envy! Your star is rising all over the world. You are becoming a renowed artist, darling. And all because of what I've done for you."

He watched her carefully while she spoke, seeing for the first time what his passions had blinded him to all along. "What you've done for me?"

"Exactly! I've made you, darling. Without me, you would be nothing, wasting away your talent painting rocks and trees."

Darren saw evil, dark and ugly, on her face, and had recognized it for what it was. Rebecca had thought that she could possess him and use him for her own benefit, as well as mold his art to suit her own tastes.

"And made yourself richer, too!"

"Of course," she said with an eloquent shrug. "What other reason would I have for spending so much time with one of my artists?"

"Love, I had thought."

"Of course I love you, darling," she said quickly.

"Do you? Or do you love the money and the publicity?"

"Please, Darren darling, you're acting like a temperamental artist. Look at what I've given you. Look at how well you paint now. See the power in your work. You never had that before. I gave it to you!"

"Gave it to me?" he asked, staring at his latest painting. He looked at it for several seconds and found himself hating it passionately. "No, Rebecca, what you've done is to corrupt me. What I paint now is nothing!" Darren raised his arm and pointed to the completed canvas. "What I see before me is emptiness!"

Staring at the painting, Darren began to despise both it and himself. Determinedly, he lifted the painting from the easel. Holding it out toward her, he slowly shook his head.

"You call this great art, do you?" he asked angrily.

"No. I don't call that great art. I made it great art. I made that worth fifteen thousand dollars more than it would have been without me!"

"Then sell it! It's the last money you'll make off me!"

"We have a contract," Rebecca had reminded him in a level voice.

"You've used me for two years, Rebecca. I was an easy target for you, wasn't I? When did you see the dollar signs? When you first met me and realized I was just a down-home country boy?" Darren took a deep breath and shook his head adamantly. "You played with my emotions and I let you. You changed my art and I didn't stop you. But now I'm doing just that! We have no contract. We have nothing!"

"But we do, darling, we do," she whispered, walking toward him, smiling confidently, sure of her power over him.

Darren stepped back, his mind truly clear for the first time since he'd met her. "If you represent yourself as my agent after today, I will see you in court."

With that, he ordered her out of his studio. Twenty-four hours later he closed the studio, left New York City, and never returned.

In the four years since he had ended that ill-fated romance, Darren had rediscovered the purpose of his artistic life, and at the same time had become aware of how much the land around him was changing.

The advances of civilization were taking their toll on the land that he loved to paint. Air pollution from the big cities was drifting over the Rockies, certain breeds of animals were dying out, and major corporations were trying to gain drilling rights for oil and gas.

Soon there would be no more natural lands to paint. Everything would be destroyed. The wildlife that was so much a part of the Southwest would be gone.

Darren sensed that part of the reason for his sudden concern for the environment had been a result of Rebecca Charlow's abuse. He knew, too, that he had once taken the land for granted. When he had returned to Santa Fe, he had realized that he could no longer use the land the way Rebecca had tried to use him and his art. He must somehow repay nature for giving him so rich a subject for his palette.

In the past, he'd viewed environmental organizations as insignificant. After his return, he'd come to see just how important they were, and had devoted whatever free time he had to one group in particular.

For the past four years, Darren's life had revolved around his work as an artist and his work as a naturalist. He had no other time to give, and he had preferred it that way.

Then why did I take Lea to dinner? he asked himself, shaking off his bitter memories of Rebecca Charlow.

Because she's different. Darren sensed that Lea was very different. Her beauty beckoned to him, and when he'd looked into her hazel eyes, he'd glimpsed a strange vulnerability that was part strength, part emotion. He sensed, too, that Lea was not the type of woman to use a man.

As the sun rose in all its majesty, Darren found that his anticipation of seeing Lea again was growing stronger. Although she was a vastly different woman from Rebecca Charlow, caution tempered his anticipation, perhaps because of the unhappy memories of Rebecca.

Although, Darren admitted ruefully as he thought of his evening with Lea, *there was no caution when I kissed her last night, or asked her to spend the day with me today.*

The day passed with a speed that frightened Lea. From the moment Darren had picked her up at the hotel, time itself seemed to have accelerated, while Darren drove her everywhere, pointing out sights that more often than not took her breath away.

Despite this being her third trip to the area, everything that he was showing her was unfamiliar. Her total concentration with the project had kept her confined to the valley for most of the time she was in New Mexico.

Even when she'd had the free time, she had not been interested in anything other than the valley and her plans. But with Darren pointing out all the sights, Lea realized how much beauty she had missed.

They drove in his Land Rover for hours, usually along the dirt roads that crisscrossed the federal land preserves. At two, Darren drove onto low-lying flat-lands nestled at the base of a high, cloud-capped mountain. There he took a cooler from the back of the vehicle, and he and Lea shared a light lunch, complete with a half bottle of California Chablis.

After lunch, her tour continued, and Lea let the me-lodic quality of Darren's voice lull her senses. He showed her places that looked as if they'd never been trod upon by man. The sights affected her deeply, and served to make her even more aware of the project's importance.

She wanted to make the community a part of the land, not the land a part of the community. Lea knew that it only took one small mistake to destroy the pre-carious balance between nature and civilization, and she would never willingly allow that mistake to occur.

By late afternoon, they headed back toward Santa Fe, but a few minutes later Darren pulled to the side of the road and gazed at Lea. "Do you want to go back to the hotel now?" he asked.

Lea returned his gaze as she thought about the tone of his voice. "Or?"

"Have dinner with me at my place?"

Lea knew her answer had to be the hotel. It had to be! "Dinner sounds good," she answered, not believing the words that issued from her lips.

Darren smiled, put the vehicle into gear, and started off again. After fifteen minutes, he turned off the main highway and onto a rocky dirt road that rose upward along the mountainside. The Land Rover's suspension absorbed the less-than-smooth surface and, after a few miles, Darren turned onto a gravel drive.

A few moments later, a house built on the side of the mountain came into view. It was set a short distance from a small grove of juniper pines, and Lea instinctively knew it fitted Darren perfectly.

The house was a medium-size two-story ranch, with a stone-and-wood facade. It was simple and elegant, and her trained eyes knew it was at least fifty years old. To the left was another structure, very different from the house. Its walls were made of reddish brown adobe clay, and on its flat roof was the dome of a huge skylight.

When Darren stopped the Land Rover and shut off the engine, he turned to Lea. He saw the way her eyes took in every detail of the house and, several minutes later, saw an approving nod of her head.

"It's lovely," she told him.

"It is." Then he stepped down from the vehicle, walked around to the passenger side, and helped Lea down.

Once inside the house, Lea was as impressed with the interior as she had been with the exterior. The inside was done in wood and plaster, except for a large fieldstone fireplace dominating one wall of the living room. The floor was of highly polished oak. The large dark beams crossing the ceilings were hewn from thick pine trees.

The walls were painted in soft earth tones. Only a few unpretentious paintings hung on the walls. After seeing the living room, and the dining room that was separated from it by a wide doorway, Lea followed Darren into the spacious kitchen.

A double gas range was set into one wall, with wide butcher-block counters on both sides of the range. The sink was set into another butcher-block counter beneath a generous window. Across from the long counter was the refrigerator, in an alcove created by pine cabinets. In the center of the kitchen was a work table; it too was a butcher block. Three feet from large sliding glass double doors was a round, polished-wood table. Outside the glass doors, Lea saw a wide cedar deck overlooking the mountain slope.

"You have a lovely home. Peaceful, too," she told Darren.

"That it is," Darren replied. "Why don't you go onto the deck and enjoy the view? I'll only be a few minutes," he told her as he headed toward the refrigerator.

"Can I help?" she asked, turning to him.

Darrent shook his head. "You're on vacation."

For an instant, Lea's mood darkened with the thought of her lie, but she forced herself to smile at him. "I really don't mind."

"Outside!" he commanded.

As Lea opened the sliding door, his question stopped her. "Wine or club soda?"

"I'm not a big drinker. Club soda."

"I'll be out in a minute."

With that, Lea stepped onto the deck. After crossing it, she leaned on the high railing and looked out at the panorama of mountains against the azure sky.

It was a lovely and relaxing scene, one which Lea allowed herself to enjoy fully while refusing to dwell on the guilt that his words had evoked.

If anything comes of this, I'll tell him the truth, she promised herself. Then she shook her head. *How can I tell him, and not endanger the project...or my own job?*

A few moments later, while she still wrestled with the rising conflict within her, Darren joined her on the deck. In his hands were two glasses filled with crystal-clear sparkling water. After handing her one, he turned to look at her profile.

"You're a lovely woman, Lea."

His simple statement caught her off guard and, against her wishes, her body tensed. She tried to say something appropriate, but words failed her.

Darren slowly raised his hand. When he cupped the side of her face, he let go a pent-up breath. "Is it so hard to accept a compliment?"

Lea closed her eyes for an instant. When she opened them, her free hand covered his. "Yes," she whispered truthfully. Darren withdrew his hand, and Lea reluctantly let it go.

"Then let me change it from a compliment to the truth. The truth is, Lea, you are a beautiful woman."

"Darren—"

"I hope you like steak," he said quickly, cutting off whatever she was about to say.

"I do. Darren, why are we here?"

"To have dinner."

"That's not what I mean," she whispered, staring openly at him.

"Must there be a reason for everything?"

"There usually is."

"In that case," Darren said, his eyes unblinking, his voice level and steady, "I think you know the reason we're here as well as I do."

Before she could respond, Darren's expression softened. "Would you like to see my studio?"

Lea's sigh was loud. "I'd love that."

Darren put his glass on the deck's railing and took Lea's and did the same. Then he took her arm and led her down four steps to the ground.

They crossed the hundred feet to the adobe studio in silence, with Lea intensely aware of the touch of his strong hand on her arm. When Darren opened the door and led her inside, Lea's breath caught.

The large skylight illuminated the studio with the late afternoon's soft light in such a way that it seemed as if they were standing outside. In the center of the studio, directly beneath the skylight, was Darren's easel. Resting on the wooden tripod was a draped canvas. Near it was a rolling work station filled with brushes, tubes of paint, and metal cans. Bundles of rags were stored on a lower shelf.

She walked toward the covered painting, but stopped several feet from it. Something about the way it was hidden from her sight compelled her to want to see it. "May I?" she asked as she reached toward the easel.

"No," Darren whispered.

Lea's hand stopped in midair as the same tension that had filled her the day before gripped her once again. She turned her head to glance at him, her eyes clouding at his single word. "I...I didn't mean to pry."

"It's not ready to be seen," he told her in a softer voice. "Not yet," he added.

Lea let her hand fall to her side. Then she smiled at Darren in acceptance. When she turned from him, she looked to her left. Leaning against the wall was a row of completed paintings. To Lea's eyes, each one was a masterpiece. The paintings were all variations of the same theme—the mountains, the animals, and the people who inhabited the land.

"You're a very talented artist," she told him, her voice tinged with wonder.

"Thank you," he replied, seeing the look of appreciation in her eyes.

For the next fifteen minutes, Darren was silent as Lea scrutinized the paintings lining the far wall. He began to feel the stirrings of a new desire, desire to capture more than just her face on canvas. He wanted to recreate the beauty of her entire form, a beauty that was so apparent to his own eyes.

"It'll be dark soon," he told her when she stopped to examine the last of the paintings. "Why don't we go back so I can cook, and you can watch a mountain sunset."

Lea turned to him, her mind awash with unspoken emotions. His paintings had affected her deeply; never had she seen such delicate work combined with such mastery over paint and canvas. When she looked at the pictures, she felt as though she were seeing the real thing, not just brush strokes. Animals came alive; mountain peaks looked awesome and distant; she could almost taste the cold, thin air at their summits.

Silently, not trusting herself to speak, Lea walked to him. An instant later, she lifted herself up on the balls of her feet and kissed his cheek lightly. "Thank you."

Darren looked at her, his gaze sweeping across her face. "For?"

Lea turned. She raised her arm, gesturing toward the paintings. "For sharing them with me."

"You're welcome," Darren said, his voice so low she almost didn't hear him.

Dinner had ended twenty minutes before, and Lea and Darren were again standing on the deck. The night sky was ablaze with stars; a three-quarter moon hung just above one towering mountain peak.

Both Lea and Darren were more than a little aware of each other, and of the special feeling that enveloped them like a cocoon. No words were needed, no make-do conversation. Just their being at this spot, at this time, was enough for both of them.

Lea felt at ease in the afterglow of a delicious meal and two glasses of a deep red Médoc wine. Darren's closeness did not disturb her, but she was conscious of tingling sensations whenever his arm or hand brushed against her. There was a recurring tightness in her body, not an unpleasant phenomenon, but not quite comfortable either.

"It's been a very nice day, Darren," she said, breaking the silence at last.

"It has been," he agreed, turning to gaze down upon her upturned face. The reflection from the moon lent a silvery glow to her light complexion and accented her large eyes.

While she gazed up at him, Lea's body reacted to him as if with a will of its own. Her mouth went dry under his penetrating stare.

She watched, unable to move, as he lowered his lips toward her. An instant later, their mouths met. Lea's low cry did not escape her throat, but the sudden explosion of passion shook her to her very core.

In the space of a single heartbeat, all her control fled. She returned his kiss with an ardor that took her by storm.

Her mouth softened even as her lips pressed hungrily against his. When she felt the probing entrance of his tongue, she greeted it willingly with her own. His arms encircled her, drawing her closer to him. She welcomed the heat radiating from him, as well as the feel of his strong, lean body on hers.

Her hands were on his back, pressing into its wide expanse. Her heart was beating like a trip-hammer, and her head spun dizzily when she tried to breathe. When her legs threatened to give out, she realized at last what was happening.

Finding one small thread of self-control, Lea pulled her mouth from Darren's and turned her face against his chest. She felt the warmth of his breath on the top of her head, and heard the strong beating of his heart.

His hands caressed her back gently, but her own hands were deathly still. "Too soon," she whispered.

Darren moved so quickly that she was taken by surprise to find herself staring up at him. His hands were on her shoulders now, his eyes blazing from beneath narrowed lids.

"Too soon for what?" he asked, his voice like a growl. "What's happening to us is right. I want you, Lea. And you want me." With his last word, he lowered his mouth toward hers.

Lea tore her mouth from his and pulled herself away from Darren. Shaking her head emphatically, she continued to battle with her emotions. Desire, need, and a myriad of other feelings stirred maddeningly in her mind, but her anger at his overconfident egotistical statements held them at bay.

The magic of the night had been irrevocably shattered, and for the first time since she'd met him, he had sounded like all the other men she'd known, the men who acted as if they were in charge of her mind and body and understood her needs better than she.

The unexpected outpouring of her desire still flooded her senses, confusing her thoughts. But even that paled at the knowledge of the danger in which she had placed herself. The very desires Darren had awakened and brought out in her could destroy her life's work. Her dreams, and the goals she had worked so hard to achieve, were almost within her grasp. But she sensed intuitively that all her hopes could be stripped away from her because of her unsuspected weakness for this self-assured artist.

"I thought you might be different. I was wrong," she said, her voice tight, her words accented by anger. "You haven't the slightest understanding of what I want or need—only what you want!"

Crossing her arms on her chest, Lea dug her fingers harshly into her upper arms. Her voice, when she spoke again, turned to ice. "Take me back to my hotel!"

Darren stood stiffly under her verbal onslaught, caught by surprise at her abrupt change of mood. His momentary confusion soon turned to anger. He stared at her for several seconds, ignoring the beauty illuminated by the silver cast of the moon, until at last he had controlled his temper.

"And you don't know what you want, either," he told her. Then he shook his head. "I think the hotel is the best place for you tonight." With that, he started from the deck.

Lea followed silently, her anger offset by his own clipped words. But, she knew that what she had done had been the right thing. *Everything is happening too quickly!*

An irrational, untimely memory of her feelings mere minutes before returned to haunt her: it was her thoughts about the future she had felt in his arms. She shook her head in protest. *No! I'm not prepared to sacrifice my life for you,* she said silently to Darren's broad back.

Chapter Four

The ten-mile trip to the hotel was made in a deafening silence. The only sounds were those of the tires on the road and the heavy, controlled breathing of the vehicle's two occupants.

When Darren dropped her off, he didn't say goodbye. He simply made a quick U-turn and drove away, leaving Lea to stare at the departing vehicle and wonder how she could have been so badly mistaken about someone.

She walked slowly into the hotel, going directly to her room. Once inside, she moved aimlessly about. After taking off the clothing she'd worn all day and changing into a nightgown, she turned on the television, settled into a chair, and stared at the set.

It took several moments before she realized what she was watching—a PBS documentary on Van Gogh. Acting quickly, Lea shut the television off. "I don't need to learn anything else about artists," she told the blank screen.

Lea glanced at the bed, wanting to be able to go to sleep, but she knew that would not be an escape offered so easily to her. Instead, she walked to the desk and opened up her attaché case.

She withdrew a sheet of paper, and began to look it over. Five minutes later, as she reviewed the two years of work she'd already put into the project, she was able to free her mind of thoughts of Darren.

This trip to Santa Fe marked the beginning of the third and most important phase of the design and development of the project. The first two years had been spent in accumulating data, completing topographic surveys, and mapping out both the sanitary and storm sewerage, electric, water, and gas distribution plans.

She had been on the scene when all the drainage, water flow, and water pressure tests had been secretly conducted, and had assisted in the roadway classification survey. On her own, she had handled the building characteristic design survey, and the innovative landscape features survey.

Lea had compiled a full dossier of possible designs for the community, and had documented the necessity of utilizing her original designs and concepts for a project of this magnitude. She had also worked out three alternative design ideas in case her original plans were not as viable as she anticipated.

But Lea also knew that anything less than her original plans would not be good enough for her, or for the community. Lea's designs were for a mixed community of senior citizens and young families. The senior citizens who moved to the valley would be the type of people who could not stand for the confinement and inactivity of conventional retirement. In the valley, they would be a small but important sector of community life, who worked with the young children while their parents were at work themselves, rather than just wasting their remaining years in a retirement village.

It was not an unheard-of idea, but it was an untested one. The community itself would be self-sufficient, and have all the amenities, as well as the educational and recreational facilities necessary to enjoy life.

Offices would be constructed so that work would only be a short distance from any home. The overall design of the community was set up to make the residents prefer to walk to most locations in the community, rather than to drive. It was an innovative plan with far-reaching consequences. The overall architectural design was one that blended the buildings into the landscape, making one complement the other.

But as she flipped another page, Lea realized—though not for the first time—the importance of the project. For if it succeeded, it could pave the way for major changes in community living. What she desired so strongly was the very thing she had learned from her mother, and from life itself. She needed to use her talent to make people live with, and not just use, the land they inhabited.

This project was her chance to make her hopes and dreams come true, and she would allow nothing to stand in her way. "Nothing! Not even you, Darren Laird," she whispered as she put her paperwork back in the attaché case and closed it.

Ten minutes after she slipped beneath the covers of the bed, she willed her conflicting emotions to ease, and fell asleep.

After a sleep filled with the haunting images of Darren's face, Lea rose early, showered, dressed, and had a light breakfast. When the waitress brought her the check, she also brought the box lunch that Lea had ordered. After leaving the hotel's dining room, Lea stopped at the front desk, where she found a message waiting for her. The message from Jim Stetman—the rancher who had sold her company the land for the project—was a request for her to meet with him this morning.

She called Stetman to find out what he wanted, but he was unavailable to come to the phone. She told the person on the other end of the line that she would drive out, and to please let Mr. Stetman know. After gathering her attaché case and camera, Lea left Santa Fe in her rented car. Thirty-five miles later, about halfway between Santa Fe and Taos, Lea turned onto a side road, and followed it to the wooden gate of the Stetman Ranch.

Throughout the forty-minute trip, Lea had done her best to think only of the project, but she had not been completely successful. The disturbing memories of the previous night's argument with Darren constantly impinged on her thoughts. Her desire to feel his lips on hers again was tempered by the knowledge of the danger he represented to her career.

Parking the car at the end of the circular drive, and thrusting aside her personal life for the moment, Lea went to the front door of the sprawling ranch. She knocked, and a moment later the door was opened by a dark-haired young woman.

Less than two minutes after Lea was led into the study, Jim Stetman joined her in the dark paneled room. "Mornin', Miss Graham," he greeted in his Southwestern accent.

"Good morning, Mr. Stetman."

"Sorry I wasn't able to answer your call; had a slight problem in the stables. But I do appreciate y'all coming out here so quickly," he added as he sat down at his desk.

"Is there a problem?" Lea asked.

"There might be. Seems one of them conservation groups got wind that I sold the land."

"How?" Lea asked quickly, sensing danger in his words.

"Damned if I know…. Late yesterday afternoon, a man and woman showed up asking questions about the valley."

"What did you tell them?" Lea asked apprehensively.

"Nothing. I told them it was none of their business what I did with my land."

Lea closed her eyes for a second as her mind raced with the implications of Stetman's news. She knew that their position was precarious enough without having an environmental group breathing down their backs.

"How could they have found out anything?"

"Beats me. But you have to remember that everyone knows everyone else's business in these parts. And you've had two years of free time already."

"Do they know what we're planning to do?" she asked.

"I don't believe so, but these are the same people who tried to buy the valley a few years back. The Environmental Preservation League."

Lea knew the story. Jim Stetman had inherited the ranch from his father. The valley had been part of his inheritance, but because of its distance from the ranch, and because it was almost completely surrounded by national and state preserves, it had never been used for anything.

Jim Stetman had been a rancher all his life, and had made an excellent living until several years before when, amid rising costs and low beef prices, his business had fallen on hard times. That was how her firm had learned of the availability of the land near Santa Fe. Stetman had needed to sell the land in order to keep his ranch from becoming another victim of the nation's economic losses.

When the land first went on the market, a number of environmental groups had tried to purchase it and turn it into part of the state and federal park system; they had also expected Stetman to take a minimum amount of money.

He'd refused their offer, but then learned that no one else wanted to buy the land because of their fear of a confrontation with the conservationists. After an unsuccessful year, Stetman had withdrawn the public offering, and had turned to private channels.

When he'd been approached by Lea's firm, and learned that the company was not going to build expensive condominiums or manufacturing plants, he had agreed to sell them the land and to keep the deal secret until Lansing and Mitchell was ready to make the public announcement. After living all his life in New Mexico, Jim Stetman understood the importance of the sale's secrecy.

Lea knew that Jim Stetman was a decent man, and one who loved the land. He hadn't wanted to see too much change, and recognized the potential dangers both to the environment and to the people who had always lived in the area. But he was also a realist, and refused to see his own life destroyed in order to satisfy other people's needs.

"What can we do?" Lea asked at last.

Stetman shrugged his shoulders. "Not much at this point. Y'all will have to wait to see what they'll do after they find out your plans. But I would suggest that y'all speed up your work, and start getting approval for construction before they muster their forces."

"It's not that simple," Lea stated.

"Nothing ever is, but y'all are going to have to try to make it that simple," Stetman advised. "Besides, I really don't think y'all will get that much opposition from the regular people; after all, this new community will be far enough outside Santa Fe to keep it separate, but also give the local economy a boost."

Lea nodded. "Can I use your phone?"

Stetman stood. "Make yourself at home. I have to get back to work. Would y'all care for some coffee?"

Lea shook her head. "No, thank you."

A few minutes later, Lea was speaking to Robert Kanter, explaining the latest development. After she hung up the phone, her mind was no more at ease. Her boss had had no ready answers for her, but had promised to see what he could do. Then he'd told her to go ahead with her work, but to make doubly sure that she was careful with whomever she spoke to.

After leaving the Stetman ranch, Lea drove back toward Santa Fe. Seven miles outside the city, she turned onto the poorly maintained private dirt road that led to the entrance of the small valley. When she reached the end of the road, she parked her car, hung her camera around her neck, and started walking.

At the mouth of the valley—a flat entrance five hundred yards wide—Lea stopped. Uncapping the camera, she began taking picture after picture. Although she'd done this three times before, it was with a different eye and different thoughts that she captured the beauty of the valley.

The camera swung everywhere, taking in the wide, slightly hilly land. Lea had already planned every building in the valley, and the photographs she was taking were only of those places.

When she'd finished her second roll of film and loaded the third, she began shooting the sloping hills that formed a ring around the valley floor. When that roll of film was finished, Lea capped the lens of the camera and walked deeper into the valley.

All around her, trees of varying heights rose majestically skyward. Their power and beauty held her in thrall, while she thought of ways to keep as much of nature's beauty alive as possible throughout the construction.

A half hour later, Lea stood in a clearing at the center of the small valley's floor. As she looked around, she sank to the ground, enjoying the feel of the warm earth beneath her. But even as she tried to enjoy the beauty, she finally gave in to the feelings she had been holding back all morning, and at last allowed her thoughts to dwell on Darren Laird.

Lea eyed the contours of the slopes, and as she followed the rising hills, she saw the rocky outcrop from which she had nearly fallen. Her left thumb traced the outline of her index finger's broken nail, while her mind replayed the incident. She remembered, all too vividly, the fear that had turned her cold as she'd fought to hold on to the rock that was the only object between her and certain injury.

She felt again the reassuring feeling of Darren's strong hands gripping her wrists as he'd pulled her to safety. Suddenly, the powerful sensations that had struck her when she'd looked into his face for the first time returned. The memory of their first kiss in front of her hotel room door released a lance of heat within her. Then all of the previous day's events came to mind. The warm and comfortable feeling of being with him as they drove across the mountains reminded her of how she had felt throughout the day.

Her confused state made her close her eyes for a moment. When she opened them, she felt no easing of her troubled thoughts. When Darren had kissed her so passionately the previous night, she had responded with equal fervor. The warm and subtle touch of his lips had awakened a hunger she'd never been aware of before. His well-muscled chest, pressing against hers, had imparted a wondrous sense of security. His arms had held her tightly, making her a willing prisoner in them.

Why am I afraid? she wondered. Her question gave her the answer. It hadn't been what he'd said to her, or even his cocky, overconfident manner. It had been her own *fear* that had given rise to her anger when he'd spoken, a fear that her own weakness would cost her, once again, her identity as well as her career.

With a clarity of thought that she had been lacking since she'd met Darren Laird, Lea understood her fears. She was afraid of repeating the same mistakes she'd made with Richard. She was frightened that if she gave in to her emotions, she would find herself once again subservient to a man.

The possibility of having her career, her ambitions, and her goals sidetracked by her emotions was the basis for her irrational reaction to Darren; it was the very thing that had made his words seem overconfident, rather than what they were: a reflection of their needs.

I'm not afraid of him. I'm afraid of myself! This revelation did nothing to ease her torment; it served only to make her more acutely aware of her frailties.

Why did he say anything? If he hadn't— Lea cut herself off quickly, knowing that to continue with that train of thought would only lead to more frustration. The time spent at his house could have been disastrous for Lea, and she was thankful that he had spoken up and saved her from herself.

He's like all the rest. He'll use me. But even as she told herself this, she knew it wasn't true. Intuitively, she understood that Darren Laird was not like any other man she had ever met. In the short time that they'd spent together, she had seen a sensitive side of the man that had attracted her even more than his handsome looks. His inner strength was almost tangible; his confident air was no front for hidden, character flaws.

"What's wrong with me?" she asked aloud. Then her body tensed, and she worried her lower lip between her teeth. *No!* she cried silently, shaking her head at the same time. But she could not rid herself of the realization that confronted her with truth and fear.

It's too soon. It can't happen this fast! Her denials came swiftly, but she felt no confidence in them. Again, she saw Darren Laird's face, felt his arms around her, tasted his lips.

I just met him, she tried to tell herself. *How can I be falling in love with him? I don't know him.* But Lea knew she was lying to herself. She did know Darren. She knew him well enough to sense that she was falling in love with him.

"Loving someone isn't something you decide to do, it's something that happens whether you like it or not," her father had told her when she was barely a teenager and had questioned why he loved his wife, Lea's mother.

Of all her friends, Lea had been the only one whose parents both worked. For several years she had been somewhat jealous of her friends, because when they came home from school, their mother was always there for them.

Shortly after her fourteenth birthday, on a cloud-darkened afternoon, Lea had come home from school feeling lonely. When she'd entered her house in the suburbs of Washington, D.C., and gone into the kitchen to get a drink, she'd realized that her father was sitting at the table, sipping a cup of coffee.

She's stared at him in surprise, then suddenly burst into tears. It had taken Phillip Graham several minutes to calm Lea down. When he had, he'd asked her what was wrong.

"How can you love her?" she'd demanded to know. "She's always working. She's never home where she belongs!"

Her father had said nothing for a while, and then he'd taken her hands in his and smiled gently. "Some people are meant to stay at home and raise a family, others are not. You, I, and your mother would be very unhappy if she had to stay home every day instead of doing the work that makes her so special. Lea," he'd continued in a soft and patient voice, still not releasing her hands, "your mother is a unique woman, and you're a lucky young lady to have her."

"Am I?" she'd challenged, unmollified.

"Yes!" he'd insisted. "More than you know right now. And don't for a single moment think that your mother loves you any less because she works. If anything, she loves you more. She knows how hard it is on you, coming home every day to an empty house. But if she stayed at home, it would be even harder on you, because she wouldn't be the same woman."

"Wouldn't you rather have fallen in love with some-one who would stay home?" she had persisted.

Her father had smiled, and then released her hands. "God forbid," he'd said in mock horror. Then his expression had turned serious; his eyes had probed her deeply. "I hope that you will understand all of this one day. But, for now, all I can say is that loving someone isn't something you decide to do, it's something that happens to you, whether you like it or not."

"Do you like it?"

"No, Lea, I love it. And I love you." With that, Phillip Graham had taken his daughter into his arms, and held her for a long time. When he'd let her go, he'd smiled tentatively at her. "Why don't you talk to your mother about this?"

"I don't know...."

"That will be your decision," he'd said, and Lea had known that he would never mention their talk to her mother; it would be up to Lea to speak of it.

Strangely, she had felt much better after talking to her father, and never had spoken to her mother about it. She hadn't needed to after thinking about her father's advice.

Lea looked up at the blue sky, her eyes blurring from her memories. "I love you both," she whispered to all that remained of her parents—her wonderful memo-ries of the warm and loving people who had given her life, who had taught her of love before they had died in the same way they had lived: together.

All too soon, Lea became aware of her surroundings again, and especially of the reality of her vacillating feelings for Darren Laird. *Can I possibly be in love with him?* she wondered, her thoughts stronger, less afraid. In answer to her silent question, she felt her heart swell. Even though she'd met Darren less than forty-eight hours before, she knew she was indeed falling in love with him.

Suddenly, she couldn't sit still. Standing, she brushed off the dirt clinging to her jeans, and started back to her car. Fifteen minutes later, Lea pulled the car to a stop at the same place she had two days before. She felt a need to rediscover the exact location where she had first laid eyes on Darren Laird. A sudden disappointment shadowed her thoughts when she saw that Darren's Land Rover was not there. In that moment, she realized that she had been hoping subconsciously that he had returned to paint.

Shaking her head at her foolishness, Lea retrieved her box lunch and the hotel blanket from the back seat and, with her camera still hanging around her neck, searched for a level place that overlooked the valley.

After spreading out the blanket, she slipped the camera over her head and sat down. As she opened her box lunch, her eyes wandered over the valley, and the thrill of excitement returned. "It will be as beautiful when it's finished as it is now," she promised.

Darren stopped the Land Rover next to Lea's rented car. After shutting off the ignition, he sat back and stared through the windshield. He'd spent the past several hours debating with himself, challenging himself not to return to this spot. But by eleven-thirty his emotions had overruled his common sense, and he had found himself loading his equipment into the vehicle, and driving here.

Although he hadn't really expected to find Lea, he felt a surge of excitement at discovering her car.

After dropping Lea off at the hotel the night before, Darren had driven back home, his anger as strong as when it had first surfaced. Her unwarranted accusations, as well as her flaring anger, had cooled the passion that had been gripping him.

At home, his bitterness had dimmed, while the memory of sweet-tasting lips had grown strong. Because he hadn't slept at all the previous night, his tired body had refused to let his thoughts keep him awake, and within an hour of returning home, he'd fallen into a deep, dreamless sleep.

When he woke at sunrise, he'd remembered everything that had happened the day before, and even as his anger had begun to build, he'd felt the sudden onset of losing Lea before he'd won her.

Why did she react that way? he'd wondered. When he'd spoken to her, he had sensed that she felt the same way as he did. It hadn't been merely desire and passion that had made him speak, but an emotional compulsion.

Can I just let her walk out of my life? he'd asked himself. But Darren knew he couldn't force her to become a part of his life either.

After drinking two cups of strong black coffee, Darren had gone to the studio, uncovered the painting, and begun to work again. His hands had flown over the canvas, the brush adding the minutest detail until Lea's face had begun to reflect a life that transcended the image.

For three hours, Darren had lost himself in the painting. He'd refined Lea's features, made them the central focus, without disregarding any of the beauty of the valley.

When he'd finally stepped back, he knew that he had captured the very essence of Lea's beauty, and that this particular painting was one of the best, if not the very best, he had ever done.

While he'd studied both his work and the face of the woman he hardly knew, Darren had realized that he could no more let her walk away from him than he could erase her face from the canvas and his memory.

Even as he'd started to pack his equipment, he'd kept telling himself that he shouldn't be running after her. If she didn't want him, then he should leave well enough alone.

Remember Rebecca, he warned himself. "She's not Rebecca," he'd stated aloud.

Suddenly, Darren had known that he had to see her and talk to her one more time. Then if he no longer sensed the things he had last night, he would say goodbye to her, and do his best to forget her.

After putting his easel, paints, and a fresh canvas into the Land Rover, he'd gone into the house and called the hotel. He'd been informed that Miss Graham was out and had left no word as to when she would return.

Darren had hung up the phone and gone out to the vehicle. Although it had made no sense, he'd had a feeling that she might be at the valley.

He'd started driving. Twenty minutes after leaving home, Darren had stopped the Land Rover next to Lea's rented car. Shutting off the ignition, he sat back and wondered exactly what would happen when he found her.

But he could not sit still for very long and, with a determined sigh, he left the vehicle and started toward the hilltop where he instinctively knew she would be. A few minutes later Darren stopped. He gazed at Lea's back for several long moments, taking in the subtle lines of her figure, before he started forward again.

Sitting beneath the warm midday sun, Lea absently ate cold chicken. Her thoughts dwelled solely on the future and what it held in store for the people who would one day be living here. She was totally engrossed in her reverie and it took several seconds for her to realize that the sound she was hearing was boots on the hard-packed rocky earth.

Turning suddenly, a piece of chicken held between two fingers, she looked up to see Darren standing six feet away. Her eyes widened; her breath caught. For what seemed to be endlessly long hours, but in reality was only a few brief seconds, Lea stared into his face.

"Hello," Darren said in a low voice.

Chapter Five

"Hello," Lea replied at last. The single word sounded too hollow in her ears.

"Have you cooled off yet?"

"Have you?" she retorted.

"You're even more beautiful when you're angry," Darren said, but no smile softened the hard set of his mouth.

"Am I?" The tension that always seemed to mark their meetings grew thick once again.

Darren gazed at her, studying the regal lines of her face, noticing the hint of sadness in her hazel eyes. "Lea, about last night—"

"Let's forget last night." Lea said quickly, stopping him from whatever he was about to say. Her heart was again beating much too fast, and her breath was lodged somewhere between her lungs and her lips.

Darren exhaled loudly. "I don't want to forget last night."

"Please," Lea whispered, not wanting to rehash the previous night's events.

Darren nodded slowly. "For now."

When he started toward her, Lea rose quickly, brushing her hands together to rid them of any crumbs.

"I was hoping I would find you here," Darren admitted, his eyes once more wandering over the planes of her face.

"I...I was too," Lea said, her hesitant words spoken truthfully.

"Let's walk." As he spoke, he held out his hand to her.

Lea placed her hand in his. When his fingers closed securely around hers, she smiled for the first time that day.

After a few steps, Darren said in a soft voice, "We're pretty far from the tourists' beaten paths. How did you discover this place?"

Lea remained silent. She looked up at him, again aware of the importance of secrecy. At the same time, she sensed she could trust her heart and tell him the truth. Suddenly, the vacillating emotions started to drive her mad.

Lea was afraid that by telling him the truth she might hurt the project and possibly cost herself her job, spelling the end of her dreams. But the silent pleading of her heart assured her that he would understand.

Reaching her decision, Lea shrugged nervously in preparation for telling him her story, but before she could begin she saw that Darren had taken the shrug to be a wordless answer.

Darren smiled at her. "I found this place when I was a kid. I loved to follow old roads to see where they led. This isn't state or federal land, it's privately owned, but never used. I've been coming here to paint for years."

Lea's grip tightened involuntarily as she again gathered her resolve to speak the truth. "Darren, I—"

"Look!" Darren ordered, interrupting her. Lea glanced in the direction he pointed, and found herself staring at the rocky outcrop from where she'd almost fallen. Perched on the same spot as before, Lea saw the collared lizard basking its long-tailed body on the heated surface of the rock. She studied it for a moment, and saw that its head was covered with orange and yellow specks, iridescent in the sun.

"It looks so much smaller today," Lea whispered, realizing that being startled by the unexpected appearance of the lizard had made it seem quite larger than it really was.

"It's only big if you're an insect or a smaller lizard," Darren told her good-naturedly.

Lea glanced quickly at him. "I'm glad I'm not."

"So am I."

Their eyes locked, and Lea felt a sudden charge of electricity flow between them. The power of his voice was slowly breaking down the barriers she had erected for her own protection.

They started to return, but stopped before they reached the blanket. "A lot of people are afraid to come to places like this alone."

"Afraid? Why?"

Releasing her hand, Darren stepped away from her and swung his arm in a circle. "They feel small and insignificant in comparison to the mountains and the sky. They look at the beauty around them, and become afraid. To them it's cold and forbidding, not grand and magnificent." Darren gazed at the mountains in the far distance.

"The beauty of the western mountains is a stark beauty. It is power and grandeur and millions of years of growing and changing. Everywhere you look, you see something different. And yes!" he stated, his voice growing loud, "it is something to stand before in awe. But it's nothing to be afraid of."

Lea watched the animation in his face, and felt the emotions his words brought forth. She saw how deeply he loved the beauty of the land, and realized that it was that very love that combined with his talent to make him so great an artist.

"But," Darren continued in a lower voice, his eyes again resting on Lea's face, "because people fear those things which they can't control, they either leave the beauty behind, not seeing it for what it truly is, or try to change it into a reflection of what they want."

"Not all," Lea whispered.

Darren gazed at her and slowly shook his head. "No, not all."

Reeling under the impact of his gaze, Lea saw a change come over him. Her heart fluttered erratically, and her stomach felt like a butterfly trapped in a net.

"I guess I knew it when I first saw you," Darren said in a husky voice. His eyes took in every feature of her face, moving quickly yet caressingly.

Lea's mouth was dry. "Knew?" she asked quietly.

Darren sighed, but did not respond to her question. "Do you know that your eyes change color depending on the background? Right now they're predominantly green, like the tree behind you."

All Lea could do was hesitantly nod her head. Every movement she made, every breath she took, made her realize how tautly her nerves were being stretched by Darren's closeness.

The silence between them grew more intense. A myriad of thoughts raced through her mind, but only one sent an alarm ringing in her head. She tried to cast the thought from her, knowing that what Darren had spoken of was their feeling toward each other, not the reason she had come to the valley.

When Lea could take no more of his burning gaze, she turned away from him and looked up at the sky. "Darren, you said you 'knew it' the first time you saw me. What did you know?"

Her blood pounded in her ears even as a cool breeze rose to tug at her hair. His hand fell on her shoulder and she almost jumped at the touch. A few second later his other hand came to rest on her other shoulder, and she felt the heat radiating from them, through her shirt and into her skin.

His hands gripped her, and he turned her to face him. She was free from his touch for only a moment before his hands returned.

Gazing up into his eyes, she moistened her lips with the tip of her tongue and waited for him to speak.

"I see the answer to your question in your eyes, Lea," he told her in a smooth, deep voice. Confidently, he drew her to him, his hands clutching her shoulders as his mouth descended toward hers.

Their lips met and Lea's heart stopped beating. Slowly, it began to thump, so loud that she was sure the entire world could hear.

Then her fear of Darren's discovering who she was caused her to think of only Darren and herself. The entire world was too much for her to deal with.

Her mouth parted at the gentle insistence of his tongue, and as he entered her mouth, his hands slipped from her shoulders to glide around her back and pull her firmly to him.

Lea's arms circled him, her fingertips kneading the tense, rippling muscles as she returned the passion of his kiss with her own rising desire.

As her blood thundered in her ears, Lea drew her lips from his and looked up into Darren's face. "I do know," she told him, her eyes misting.

"And it's not too soon?" he asked, his gaze never leaving hers.

"Last night was too soon. Last night I didn't understand what was happening to us," Lea admitted, lifting her hand to stroke his cheek. Without another word, she raised herself up and kissed him deeply. When their mouths joined, the world once again receded until it contained just her and Darren and the land.

The heat within her grew into a flaming volcano that sent tongues of fire through her. Darren's lips, hungrily devouring hers, only added fuel to the fire.

She was conscious of the way his chest was pressed against her breasts, and of her obvious desire. Deep within her, at the very center of her being, a flood of passion burst forth.

An instant later, Lea was swung off her feet. Darren's arms held her to him, one behind her back, the other beneath her thighs, as he crossed the remaining distance to the blanket she had spread out earlier.

Lea's eyes were closed, the side of her face resting at the juncture of his shoulder and neck. She smelled the heady aroma rising from his skin as her mouth opened and her lips pressed moistly into his neck.

The trip in his strong arms lasted an eternity but, finally, she was lowered to the ground and felt the blanket against her back. When at least he released her and drew his arms free, she opened her eyes.

Darren's face filled her vision. His blue-gray eyes blazed with desire. Yet Lea knew that all it would take was one word from her to turn him from her.

The sudden fear of throwing away two years of her life for one moment of love threatened to stop her, but Lea withstood its assault. She loved him, of that she was sure. Deep within her, she felt that Darren loved her, although he had not said the words.

She continued to gaze at him. Her mouth was dry. She tried to speak, but realized she had nothing to say.

Then, slowly, she raised her arms and opened them to him, her heart once again hammering rapidly.

The azure blue sky shimmered maddeningly above Darren's head. Lea closed her eyes to control the dizziness. But the fear she had been fighting returned. Then Darren's mouth was on hers again, and the fear fled under his touch.

Her hands drew him closer; the kiss turned into a passionate explosion that robbed her of her strength. Opening her eyes as they kissed, she saw only the endless depths reflected within Darren's.

Suddenly, she wanted to draw back, but his strong arms held her tightly. Then his hands were moving over her, sending waves of molten lava rippling from wherever they touched.

As it had happened the other night, her mind and body fought a battle. Logically, she knew this was too much too soon, but her heart would not heed her mind. The kiss deepened and a low moan emerged from deep in the back of her throat, mingling with all the other sounds of the valley.

Then his lips were gone, and she was again gazing up at him. She saw passion and desire written on Darren's face. A heartbeat later, his hand stroked her cheek until she gripped it with her own and brought his palm to her mouth. She kissed the tender skin softly while another wave of desire shook her senses.

Her gaze never left Darren's. As she tasted the sweetness of his skin, the last dam of her resolve broke, and she was no longer able to hold back. In an abandoned moment, while the forces of their needs and desires flowed through them, Lea saw in his face that her emotions were being mirrored within him—that he did love her. She knew then that when the time was right to tell him about herself and the valley, he would understand why she had waited.

Then his lips were on hers again, and her very being turned to liquid fire. The warm, wonderful sensation of her breasts pushing against his chest with each ragged breath she drew was dizzying. She could not control her hands as they roamed freely along the well-defined contours of his back.

Unexpectedly, another fiery burst of passion overwhelmed her, but it ended abruptly when Darren pulled away. Lea's mind spun madly; her hands reached out for him. Then his lips were on her skin again, kissing gently along the sensitive base of her throat. His short beard only added to the tingling sensations of his lips.

Lea's hands moved of their own accord to weave through his soft, wavy hair until she grasped the strands and raised his face to her lips. Her mouth covered his, and she kissed him deeply once again.

Moments later, when her lips were free, she stared into his smoldering eyes and knew that they had crossed whatever boundaries had been separating them. Never before had she felt such an unbearable need for someone; never had she been so willing a prisoner to her passions, helpless to stop herself from giving her love to Darren, and not a little afraid that she was making a mistake.

Darren gazed into Lea's smoky eyes and knew that he would not be able to hold himself back any longer. Her fingers were still wound in his hair, and he could feel the hard peaks of her breasts pressing into his chest. His gaze moved everywhere on her face, taking in every beautiful line, studying every nuance of every gesture she made.

He was totally lost in her, and had no regrets. Desire pulsed within him, but it was a gentler sensation of warmth that guided him onward. His need for Lea was tempered by this newly discovered emotion, and he was loath to free himself from it.

Darren bent his head and again tasted the pliant, vibrant skin of her neck. Beneath his lips, a vein beat with the accelerated rhythm of her heart, and his own pulse raced to keep tempo with it. His hands slid along her sides, the artist in him caressing the perfect symmetry of her body.

When a sparkling mist of desire and need stole across his mind, he turned both of them onto their sides, and brought his mouth back to hers. While one hand caressed her back, the other swept across her narrow waist, then rose upward along her side until he cupped the fullness of her breast.

Lea's body responded to Darren's every touch, even as his heated, passionate kisses made her blood rush madly through her. But when he drew away again, she could not stop the low cry of protest that sprang from her lips.

Before the sound died, she felt his hands working on the buttons of her shirt, even as hers began to do the same with his. In a haze of unremembered movements, Lea and Darren undressed each other beneath the warm New Mexican sun and, when they were both free of their clothing, lay again within each other's arms.

Darren, feeling the blazing heat from Lea's skin, drew back to gaze at every curve. His eyes roamed unrestrained, his breathing harsh.

After tracing the soft curves of her thighs, the smooth swell of her stomach, and the fullness of her peach-tipped breasts, it was her face, and the innocence there, that held him completely.

"You are a remarkable woman, Lea Graham, and I...I'm a very lucky man."

Lea sighed, warmed by his admission. Of everything Darren could have said to her, he'd chosen the words that made her heart fill with love.

Then his lips were at the base of her throat, his beard accenting the overpowering sensations. When his hands slipped beneath the small of her back, and his mouth travelled to the peak of one breast, Lea arched her back and grasped his hair tightly, pressing his mouth harder to her.

Only the feel of his lips on her breast was real. Another low moan escaped Lea's mouth when Darren's lips slowly released her breast.

Once again her back arched when Darren's lips traveled across her skin to her other breast, lavishing it with heated, moist kisses until he took its stiffened peak within. She cried out at the pleasure he was giving her, and cried when he released the swollen tip, only to trail his lips upward again.

Passion and desire overwhelmed her until there was nothing left in the world except to await his next kiss, his next caress. His hands were strong, firm yet gentle as they journeyed along her body. His artist's fingers searched her contours, learning them as well as enjoying them.

His molten fingertips wandered across her flat stomach, sending chills to every part of her body before they dipped down to caress her inner thighs one more time.

The sounds of birds flying overhead grew loud in Darren's ears as he learned more and more about the magnificent woman he was making love to. The silken feel of her skin sent a myriad of sensations to flood his being.

His desire grew stronger, turning into an all-powerful aura that threatened to take control of him. But he refused to yield to those desires; he tore his eyes from her glowing skin and raised them to her face. Then he shifted and rose above Lea.

Lea felt a change come over them even as Darren's hands left her thighs and his eyes returned to hers. Within them she saw all she needed, and although she was under the strongest physical assault she had ever known, she believed that their lovemaking was right.

"Darren," she whispered, her mouth dry not just from her desire, but from a need to speak what was on her mind. Her breasts rose and fell under the force of every breath she took.

"It's all right, Lea," Darren said in a husky voice, reassuring Lea with both word and touch.

"Darren," she repeated, her hands going to his face. She felt the teasing touch of his beard on her palms, and another thrill of excitement raced through her. "Everything is happening so quickly—"

"Not too quickly," he cut in.

"No, not too quickly for us.... But I...I've never—"

"—had to make explanations," he said, replacing whatever words she was about to speak with his own, intuitively knowing that she was trying to explain what was happening to her. "We don't need any explanations, Lea. We have each other. From today on, we have each other. Whatever was in the past is no longer a part of our world."

"Darren," she whispered for the third time, her eyes misting as her emotions wiped away all her fears and doubts.

Then he was kissing her again, gently, softly, their lips barely touching, their bodies a hair's breadth apart. Lea felt the heat radiating between them, and even as Darren shifted once again, she did also.

An instant later he was above her, his blue-gray eyes fixed on hers, his arms slipping beneath her, lifting her to meet him.

The kiss deepened as Darren lowered himself until he was pressing fully upon her. Unable to hold back any longer, Lea arched to meet him. Even as she felt Darren's heated entrance, her legs wound around his slim hips, and her fingers dug into his back.

They were joined together with a swiftness and surety that Lea had never thought possible. Beneath the fire consuming her lay the acceptance of the love she felt for Darren, and the emotions she knew were irrevocably given.

Lea felt Darren deep within her very core as they locked together in a powerful embrace of love; they were frozen in time. Darren held her close to him, neither moving nor withdrawing. Finally, as the heat within her increased, Darren began to move slowly. His hands were secure beneath her, guiding her as his hardness swelled within her. Lea was once again aware of everything: the ground beneath the blanket, the warm sunshine, the birds flying across the valley, and most importantly, she was aware of Darren, as he lifted her toward the magnificent blue heavens.

Darren was lost in the beauty that surrounded him. Lea's warmth and love and body were the refuge that he had needed for so long. It gave him the strength to merge with her, to join her so that they would become one.

With Lea's legs locked around his hips, and the rigid tips of her breasts almost piercing the skin of his chest, Darren succumbed to the wonder of the woman, and the delight of their lovemaking. Her fingernails dug into the muscles of his back, but all he felt were sparks radiating through his skin. The scent that rose from her skin and hair was a perfume that he would never forget, and never wanted to forget.

Then his lips covered hers, and their tongues danced together as their bodies continued to follow the rhythm that their hearts dictated until, at last, Darren felt Lea tighten around him, her back arching and her fingers pressing deeply into his skin.

Lea's surprised cry sounded the instant their lips parted, and all she could do was hold on to Darren as the volcano that he had awakened erupted within her depths, turning her racing blood to lava. Then they were floating above the small valley, above the tall pine trees and the powerful yet smoothly rolling hills and mountains.

They stayed aloft for eons, locked within an embrace that excluded everything but themselves. Their eyes were open, drinking in each other's face. Their breathing, ragged and forced, was as much in sync with their beating hearts as was their awareness of each other and the love they had lavished and shared. But at last, when the silky cloud of their passions eased, and their breathing returned to normal, they returned to the valley, to lie within each other's arms, listening to the beating of their hearts.

Lea was perched on the same rocks she had been on the previous day. This time she was not worried about being startled and falling. Her mind was filled with wonder; her thoughts centred on Darren, who, thirty feet from her, was working on the clean canvas he'd taken from the back of the Land Rover a half hour before.

Although she knew she should feel guilty at her earlier, wanton behavior, all she was aware of was the warm feeling of being loved and needed.

She was still under the effects of their wonderful lovemaking, and her body was warm inside, as was her skin, caressed by the afternoon sun. The real world had not yet impinged on her thoughts, and Lea kept reality at bay for a while longer.

Turning, she studied Darren as he worked. The sun illuminated his mane of dark hair. His beard was a healthy contrast to his tanned skin. His eyes were fixed on the canvas, and even at this distance, she sensed the intensity of his concentration.

He worked bare-chested, wearing only his boots and jeans. His muscles rippled as he made sweeping strokes with the brush across the canvas. Lea felt another tingle of excitement. Suddenly she wished she too could paint, so that she could capture the essence of the man as she saw him now.

Then she smiled, turned, and picked up the camera she'd taken to the rocks with her. She uncapped the lens and lifted the camera, focusing it on Darren. Looking through the viewfinder, she could see the sunlight gleaming on his skin, magnified by the light sheen of moisture that filmed his torso.

She took picture after picture, centering most of them on his face, until she ran out of film. After she put her camera away, she looked down into the valley again and lost herself to its beauty and her visions of what it would one day become.

Soon her eyes returned to Darren, and her thoughts to the passionate lovemaking they had shared. Although Lea did not consider herself an experienced woman of the world, she did know that what was growing between her and Darren was something seldom found by two people, and even more seldom kept.

That she loved him, she had no doubt at all—not any longer. She believed, also, that he loved her, although neither of them had admitted this aloud. Yet she didn't think those words were necessary. She believed that, like their lovemaking, when it was time they would give voice to their love.

Sighing, Lea leaned back against the rocks and closed her eyes, letting the gentle rays of the sun kiss her face.

She tensed suddenly as a disturbing thought intruded on her contentment. *What will happen tomorrow?*

Lea wasn't wondering about twenty-four hours from now, but about all the days following this one. There was only one move she had to make. She had to tell Darren the truth about why she was here.

When she had tried to tell him earlier, he hadn't really let her. But, she admitted, she hadn't forced him to listen, either. Perhaps it was because she was very much aware of how Darren felt about the land.

But I will tell him soon, she promised herself. Then she pushed away those dark thoughts and continued to bask in the sun.

Behind her, Darren went on with his work. He'd been completely oblivious of her photographing him, and if he'd known, it wouldn't have made any difference. An hour after he'd begun to paint, he put his brushes down and looked at what he'd done.

Darren smiled to himself because the lingering feelings that had stayed with him since he and Lea had made love had lent a swiftness and surety to his brush that had been lacking for so long. After looking over what he'd done thus far, he turned to look at Lea. Her head was tilted back, her shoulder-length hair brushing the top of the rocks. Her profile set his blood to rushing again, and he could not tear his eyes from her for several long minutes.

After they had made love, Darren had felt restless. Although he wanted to hold her to him, caress and kiss her endlessly, he hadn't been able to do so for long. Instead, he had found his fingers itching to hold a brush, and his mind bent on capturing his emotions on canvas.

He'd sat up and begun to speak, trying to explain his sudden need to paint. Before he'd finished a sentence, Lea had silenced him with a gentle finger across his lips.

"It's all right," she'd whispered. When she'd smiled, he had seen that she was speaking truthfully. He'd stood and gazed down at her unclad beauty, and felt his heart swell at the sight.

His passions had stirred again, but Lea, seeing what was happening, had pulled the blanket over her. Her eyes had glowed mischievously. "You wanted to paint, remember?" she'd teased, her eyes growing smoky again as she favored him with a yearning look. But behind her capricious teasing had been the understanding of who—and what—he was.

Darren had dressed quickly, except for donning his shirt, and had unloaded his equipment from the Land Rover. Then he'd set it all up at the very spot where he'd been working the other day.

As he did this, Lea had dressed and walked over to the rocks. Within moments of her departure, he had lost himself to the canvas.

Darren drew his eyes from Lea, and glanced at his painting. He was satisfied with what he'd done so far, and sensed that any further work would be neither as spontaneous nor as good.

Turning away from the easel, Darren cleaned the brushes and put away his equipment. He picked up his shirt from the blanket, and put it on before joining Lea where she sat on the rocks. Tenderly, he covered her hand with his.

When she felt Darren's touch, Lea opened her eyes and looked at him. Her warm smile greeted him, and her heart beat stronger. "Finished?"

"For today," he said as his hand gripped hers. "Lea...I'm very glad I met you," he whispered, leaning toward her and kissing her gently.

This time there were no startling sparks of fire, or random bursts of passion; instead, a slow glow suffused Lea and, when their lips parted, her breath eased out in a whispering sigh.

"So am I."

"What would you like to do with the rest of the afternoon?"

Lea's eyes roamed across his face. She freed her hand from his and raised it to stroke his cheek. "Whatever, as long as it's with you."

Chapter Six

Lea and Darren spent the afternoon walking along the rarely trod natural trails of the hills, feeling as one with nature itself. When the sun descended in the west, painting the mountains in breathtaking pastel hues, Lea, in her rented car, followed Darren to his house. There they worked together in the kitchen preparing a light dinner, which they ate on the cedar deck as day turned into night and the peaceful loving between them continued.

"I know why you paint what you do," Lea said after finishing a cup of coffee. "But don't you have the desire to paint other things?"

Darren gazed at her, his eyes probing deeply into hers. "What other things?"

Lea shrugged. "I don't know."

"Neither do I. Oh," he said with a half smile and a shrug, "I have painted other things—cities, people in the cities, inanimate objects, as well as having experimented with abstracts. But I've learned that what I love to paint is right here, all around me. I have no desire to become a visionary such as—a Picasso or Kandinsky."

As he spoke the names, his voice changed, and Lea detected a trace of bitterness. "I've offended you, haven't I?" Lea asked.

Darren shook his head quickly. "No, not you. But there were others who wanted to use my talent, to change it for their own profits."

"I'm sorry," Lea whispered.

Darren laughed suddenly. He reached out to her, his hand palm up, waiting for her to meet him halfway. When she complied, his fingers curled around her smaller hand comfortingly.

"Don't be sorry. If it hadn't happened, I wouldn't know what I really wanted in my life."

"And you know now?" The question was barely a whisper. Lea's heart beat slowly; her breath came haltingly.

"I know now," Darren replied. "You are part of what I want in my life."

Desire flared, but it was tempered by the gentle love that had been born that very afternoon. "I never thought so much could happen so quickly," Lea said, her fingers exerting pressure on his. "But it did. What else do you want out of life?" she asked, holding back her sudden need to feel him against her again.

"Not a lot," Darren admitted. Then he stood, bringing Lea to her feet with him. He walked to the railing of the deck and slipped his hand from hers.

Lea turned to lean against the railing, her back toward the mountains, her eyes staring directly into his. The night was complete now; a multitude of stars were strewn in the heavens and the moon was almost full, illuminating the land with a pale glow.

Darren's gaze held hers, his thoughts focused on her last question. "But there are some things that I need. I need to live here, surrounded by the mountains, far enough away from the madness of the city.

"I want always to have the freedom to paint, and to see the splendor of the land and the mountains. And I want to have a family one day. I want to teach my children about the beauty of the land."

Darren's voice contained a magical quality, its vibration filling her with hope.

"And I want to keep these mountains alive!" he stated in a strong voice.

"Alive? But they are alive."

"For now. But unless people stop the advance of civilization—or is 'modernization' a better word?" he asked suddenly, his face tightening. Then he shrugged. "Lea, there aren't many places left in this country that are unspoiled. When I was born, these mountains were hardly populated. Now there are housing developments going up everywhere that land can be bought.

"The wildlife is disappearing; the land is changing, but not naturally. People aren't content to live in cities, and I can more than just understand the reasons—I can accept their desires to get away from the concrete and steel. But what I can't accept is that when they move to the countryside, they have to bring all the conveniences of the city with them."

Lea shook her head slowly. "Aren't you exaggerating, Darren? Can't you share this land with other people?"

Darren shook his head fiercely. "Share the land? I would love to, but developers don't believe in sharing the land. They believe in owning it and changing it. They can't, or won't, utilize what nature gives them. They change it to suit their own twisted ideas of life."

Lea stiffened under his bitter tirade. But she rallied to control her response. "As an architect, I've seen several communities that have been built with the environment in mind, adding to it rather than detracting from it. It is possible."

Surprisingly, Darren nodded thoughtfully. "Possible, but rarely done. Even when it is, something has to be sacrificed. Natural patterns that have been in existence for hundreds of thousands of years are changed. Something, whether plants or wildlife, is affected. No, Lea, when man takes over, things change. And I don't want to see that happen here. For me, and for the people who live in this area, the mountains around Santa Fe are our last bastion of nature." Then Darren shrugged again. "Why are we arguing? Why are we even talking about this?"

"You started," Lea said.

Darren smiled ruefully. "That is one of my bad habits."

"Are there others?" Lea asked quickly, her eyebrows lifting in mockery.

"That's something you'll have to find out for your-self," he whispered, his voice thickening as his arms stole around her and drew her close.

Their mouths came together and their hearts beat faster. When they drew apart, their breathing was forced, and the expressions on their faces echoed each other's needs and desires. No words were needed as Darren again took Lea's hand and led her into the house.

Lea awoke through the layers of sleep, returning to consciousness and the day ahead of her. As she stretched beneath the light covers, her mind refused to allow her to think of the day ahead; she found her meditations centered on Darren, and what they had shared.

A sudden thought intruded on this memory and frightened Lea so badly that she sat up, trapping the covers against her breasts as she held her arms across them. *Is that all there will ever be between us? Can we rise above the future?*

Quickly, she turned away from the haunting question.

A wave of sadness overwhelmed her. With her new-found love, and the physical and emotional need that Darren had brought out in her, was the genuine fear that what Darren felt about the mountains, and the valley in particular, could be a wedge to drive them apart.

Lea understood the vision of beauty that powered and impelled Darren to paint and to love the land, but it was that very thing that worried her, and made her slightly afraid of what the future would bring.

He will understand, Lea told herself as she tried to force herself to leave the bed. But again, she failed in this as her thoughts turned to the lovemaking they had shared the night before.

When they'd gone from the deck to Darren's bedroom, the world had once again receded, and for Lea, there had been only she and Darren. Everything that had been said on the deck had been forgotten as she gave herself to him. This time their lovemaking was slower, and Lea was able to explore Darren's body. By the time they joined together, it was with a knowledge of who they were and why they were together.

Even later that night, when Lea was about to leave, Darren stopped her and drew her to him. He kissed her deeply before releasing her. "You've made me very happy, Lea. I never expected this."

Lea smiled shyly, her eyes misting. "Nor did I."

An uncomfortable silence had fallen between them, and Lea felt as if a gate had shut. It was a vulnerable time for her; a moment that could have destroyed everything.

Nervously, she twisted the car keys in her hands, and took a deep breath. "Well...I guess I'd better go."

"I guess so," Darren replied.

But Lea hadn't turned away from him. She had stared at him, her mind screaming for her to do something...anything!

As she'd started to speak his name, Darren had whispered hers. Again they had both fallen silent. Lea had gazed at him, her eyes pleading for him to speak first.

"I'll be working all day tomorrow, but I want to see you tomorrow night. All right?" Darren had asked.

Lea's heart had beat rapidly. "I'd like that," she said.

Now Lea remembered the lonely drive back to Santa Fe, and how she'd fallen into bed, too exhausted by the long day even to think about what had really happened.

But I have to think about it now, she told herself. There was still one remaining problem. Lea realized it might just be the biggest problem in her life. As important as Darren had suddenly become, her career was equally important.

Will he be able to accept me when he knows the truth? she wondered. *Will he keep my project a secret?* Lea cut her speculation off abruptly and left the bed, knowing that to worry would solve nothing.

Lea showered quickly, dressed, and then ordered room service. As she waited for her breakfast to arrive, she went to the desk, opened her attaché case, and took out the papers.

By the time the room service attendant arrived, the desk was covered with papers, and Lea was totally immersed in her work. After signing the check, Lea buttered a hot biscuit and, with a cup of coffee in her other hand, she studied the artist's renditions of what the valley would look like when construction was completed.

As she ate and sipped her coffee, her eyes were never still. She was satisfied with the way the sketches looked, all except for the three buildings that stood out and were different from the others.

The park area was a wide, sprawling expanse of land that utilized as much of the natural surroundings as possible. The school was set at the side of a mountain. Except for the windows and the solar panels on the roof, it would appear to be an extension of the mountainside itself.

Suddenly, Lea was looking at the drawings with different eyes. She was searching for flaws, trying to spot the small inconsistencies that would make everything else look out of place.

The phone's sudden ring jarred her concentration. Putting the cup down, Lea crossed the room and picked up the phone. "Hello?"

"Lea, it's Robert," said her boss.

"Good morning, Robert."

"I don't know about that. After your call yesterday, we had an emergency meeting. I won't even begin to tell you how upset Lansing and Mitchell are."

"You don't have to," Lea told him, aware of the large monetary investment, as well as the reputation of their firm, that rested on the success of this project.

"What we've come up with is an accelerated program. We're going to have to move up our timetable by six months."

"Six months!" The two words sounded more like separate gasps.

"Sorry, but we really don't have any choice. I'll be flying out the day after tomorrow. We're going to have to file the rest of the papers, and get things moving before that conservation group has a chance to sabotage the project."

"We could try to talk with them. We could tell them what we're doing, and show them the benefits of the project," Lea suggested.

"We've taken that route before, Lea. It doesn't work."

"But—"

"Lea," Robert said in a gentle voice, "do you remember the project in Oregon three years ago?"

Lea closed her eyes. She remembered it vividly. Lansing and Mitchell had been hired by the state of Oregon to design and build a senior citizens' complex. The land the state had set aside had been on the edge of a forest preserve. Although the construction would not affect the preserve, the conservationists had fought it, saying that it would affect the life cycles of the animals in the preserve.

The group had been shown hard scientific, biological evidence that the project would not be endangering anything—trees or wildlife. But the group had refused to ease their position. The ensuing delays had cost Lansing and Mitchell a great deal of lost time and money, and the senior citizens' complex had been stalled for so long that construction costs had escalated beyond what the state could spend. All that remained of the project was the single foundation that had been laid before the group had started its protests.

Although Lansing and Mitchell had been paid their fees, the Oregon fiasco had cost them an estimated hundred thousand dollars in wasted man hours and lost commissions. It had also cost the state of Oregon half a million dollars. Lea remembered that incident all too well.

"Yes," she said aloud.

"I'll see you the day after tomorrow."

"All right, Robert."

After hanging up, Lea could only stare at the phone. A chill raced along her spine as she realized that everything would change very quickly. *I must speak to Darren and tell him the truth. I will make him understand.*

With that, Lea returned to the desk and put the paperwork into her attaché case. She suddenly settled the decision she had been agonizing over for the past two days. She would drive to Darren's house and talk to him.

Afterward she knew she would have to return and go to work. Lea had used the past week to concentrate strictly on the project's design, believing that she had ample time for the drudgery of paperwork once she returned to the office. That was all changed now that the ecology group had learned of their plans.

Her projections would have to be rechecked for accuracy. When Robert arrived the day after tomorrow, he would expect the rough draft of the completed reports to be ready, especially if they were moving the timetable ahead six months.

After picking up her purse, Lea started toward the door when the phone rang again. Shrugging her shoulders, she walked back into the room. "Hello," she said as she brought the receiver to her ear.

"Good morning," came Darren's husky voice, "did I wake you?"

"About an hour ago, you did."

"At least you haven't forgotten me," he quipped.

His jest affected Lea badly. Her fingers tightened on the receiver; her knuckles turned white. "No, never that," she whispered. There was silence on the phone for several seconds, and when Darren spoke again, she realized he had sensed something wrong in her voice.

"Are you okay?" he asked.

"Fine," she replied, struggling to keep her voice level.

"Lea, something has come up, a minor emergency. I have to go to Albuquerque, and I don't know when I'll be back."

"I...see."

"I am sorry."

"I understand," Lea told him, her voice firm. "I'm just disappointed, that's all."

"I'll make it up to you tomorrow night, I promise."

Lea smiled, although she knew he couldn't see her. "I'll hold you to that promise," she told him.

"I'll see you tomorrow," he said just before he hung up.

Once again Lea found herself staring at the phone, wondering why it transmitted so many problems. Then she exhaled softly and shook her head.

She let her purse slide from her shoulder to the floor. With a heavy sadness, she returned to the desk and started back to work.

Darren stared out the window as the last rays of the sun set on the Sandia Mountains and illuminated the low domelike cloud of pollution that hovered above Albuquerque.

Behind him, in the elegant living room, was a small group of men and women, who at first glance appeared to be an average cross section of Albuquerque's mixed population. Although they were a cross section, they were far from average.

This group had been together for eight years, and Darren was considered one of the newer members, having become involved with the Environmental Preservation League only four years before. The group was a powerful one in New Mexico, and was a force to be reckoned with at all times.

With the low hum of conversation in the background, Darren tried to concentrate on the meeting, and not on Lea. He'd arrived a half hour before, after spending the morning, and a good part of the afternoon, in his studio, refining the haunting portrait of Lea, which he'd superimposed over the valley.

Darren usually enjoyed league meetings, but tonight he wished he was somewhere else. Specifically, with Lea Graham. Yet, Randi Blake had assured Darren that this meeting was not only important, but directly concerned him.

Turning away from the window, Darren looked at the people. Randi Blake was a tall, red-headed woman who had formed the league eight years before. Her husband, Andrew, worked for the federal government—the EPA—and was privy to a great deal of advance information.

The other dozen members were all as dedicated to their ideals as were Darren and the Blakes. Darren had found all of them to be good people.

A few moments later, Randi Blake called the meeting to order. When everyone grew silent, she stepped into the center of the room. "For the past year, things have been relatively quiet. However, two days ago, Andrew came across some information that was quite upsetting. Darren,'' Randi said, speaking directly to him, "this problem is in your own backyard, so to speak. Andrew has learned that the small valley we tried to buy three years ago to donate to the park system—"

"Stetman's valley?" Darren asked in a hollow voice.

Randi nodded. "It's been sold to a land development company."

Darren's shock held him silent as he stared at Randi. His thoughts whirled, and his vision darkened. "Who?" he finally said.

Randi shrugged her shoulders. "I hope we'll find the answer to that question tonight, when Andrew gets home. He called a little while ago. He's having trouble getting into the data banks to get all the information we need, but he thinks he'll have it tonight.

"In the meantime," Randi continued, her eyes sweeping across everyone's faces, "I think we'd best start to map out a method of fighting this new development, and perhaps forcing whoever bought the valley to sell it to us."

For the next hour and a half, the members of the Environmental Preservation League discussed methods that could be used to thwart the desecration of the valley. Yet, while the members gave voice to their own methods of disrupting the construction, Darren could only sit silently as his rage grew out of control.

By the time everyone's ideas had been heard, Andrew Blake had still not returned home. At ten o'clock, most of the people started to leave, after agreeing to meet the following week, when they would have all the facts. But Darren wasn't ready to leave. He needed to find out if Andrew had learned anything from the data banks.

"I don't know what could have happened to Andrew," Randi said after everyone except Darren had gone. She went to the phone, but before she could pick it up, it rang.

A moment later, Randi smiled at Darren. "He's on his way," she told him when she hung up the phone. "Coffee?"

"Thank you."

Randi led him into the kitchen and, after he was seated at the white Formica Parson's table, she poured him a cup of coffee. When she sat across from him, her eyebrows arched in question. "Are you okay?"

Darren shrugged. "I'm not very happy with what I learned tonight."

"I know. But we'll do something about it!"

"If we can."

"We'll just damned well make sure we can. We've won more than we've lost lately," Randi reminded him.

Her statement was true, and Darren was very much aware of the reason why: money. Most of the members of the league were either well-to-do, or had the ability to raise donations when the need arose. Darren himself always donated paintings to the league. His donation was, in his own way, a payment to the land itself.

"Can you tell me anything else about this land deal?" he asked after sipping at the coffee and making an effort to calm down.

Randi exhaled slowly and shook her head. "Andrew and I went out to Stetman's place two mornings ago—

we stopped by your house, but you were gone—and asked him about the sale. He didn't deny it. In fact, he told us that it was his land, and it was none of our business what he did with it. He was pretty belligerent.''

Darren's anger abated momentarily as he thought of Jim Stetman, a man he'd known most of his life. ''Jim's not belligerent; his back was just against the wall. Actually he's a good man. But he needed money.''

''We offered him money two years ago,'' Randi countered.

''How much was it sold for?''

''Andrew's trying to get all that information.''

Darren closed his eyes and leaned back in the chair. ''This really hurts, Randi. I don't want to see that valley changed.''

''None of us does,'' she stated.

Darren opened his eyes, his anger flaring anew. ''I won't let this deal go through. If it takes my last cent, I'll stop it somehow.''

''Darren—''

Before anything else could be said, the sound of a car door closing disrupted their conversation. A moment later Andrew Blake stepped inside. Andrew was at least six inches taller than his wife, who stood five feet eleven, and he had a thin body that many people mistook for awkward. But Andrew Blake was anything but awkward. He kissed Randi on the cheek, and then looked at Darren.

''Glad you waited,'' he said as he sat next to Darren.

''What did you find out?''

Andrew shook his head slowly. ''Damnedest maze of paperwork I ever tried to look into.'' Andrew drew a small notebook from his pocket and flipped the cover up. "The land was sold two years ago to a company called American Land Designers Incorporated, for one million one hundred thousand dollars."

Randi's whistle echoed Darren's startled reaction. "No wonder Stetman wouldn't sell to us. All we offered was two hundred and fifty thousand."

Darren's eyes flicked to Randi, but returned quickly to Andrew when he spoke again. "No paperwork has been filed, other than the deed. Because it's outside of Santa Fe property, the land is under county jurisdiction rather than city. I had to sneak into the state computer to get my information."

"What else did you find out?" Darren prodded.

"Not a whole bunch. American Land Designers is a holding company, registered as a Delaware corporation—you know how easy that is to arrange, and how difficult it is to learn more about it. I picked that up from the EPA data bank in Washington, but I couldn't get any other names."

"Which leaves us pretty much in the dark!" Darren half shouted. His open hand slammed onto the tabletop and jarred the coffee cups, accentuating his statement.

Andrew was unfazed by Darren's explosion. "Not true. It'll just take us a little longer."

"But we can't do anything until we find out what plans are being made for the valley, and by whom."

"Darren, we've been working together for a long time. And the one thing we know for certain is that when prime, undeveloped land is sold, something will be built on it. Whatever is built will eventually destroy everything around it. We will find out about this company, and we will fight them until they give up and leave!"

Darren, his anger under control, stared silently at Andrew for a moment. "Whoever bought this land has over a million dollars at stake," Darren said in a low voice that still managed to echo. "They won't cave in easily."

"You sound as though you're ready to give up," Andrew accused.

Darren smiled. It was a cold smile, a smile that sent a shiver racing along Randi Blake's spine. "I don't give up, ever."

Less than a minute later, Darren stood. "Find out everything you can and let me know the minute you do."

After saying his good-byes, Darren drove from the Blake home directly to the Pan American Highway. An hour later, he was passing the Santa Fe exit, and almost turned off the highway.

But his mood was low, and his anger still high. He didn't want to inflict that on Lea. As he looked at the dashboard clock, he saw that it was after midnight.

"Tomorrow," he promised himself.

Chapter Seven

Lea pulled off the wraparound Indian print dress and threw it on top of the growing pile of discarded clothing. Frustration made her glare at her reflection in the mirror; she grimaced when she saw how hard her face looked.

Her nerves were screaming, and her stomach was in knots. She knew she was overreacting to the day ahead, but she couldn't help it. She understood that her dissatisfaction with the way she looked was caused by her need to look as good as possible when she saw Darren.

Although they were supposed to be together the forthcoming evening, Lea, after a long and lonely night plagued by introspection, could wait no longer to see Darren, talk to him.

She had spent the previous day going over her facts and figures, redefining the priorities of the construction, both for herself and for the company. She had perfected the figures so that she and Robert Kanter would have as little trouble as possible when they filed the paperwork with the state and county building commissions.

When she'd finally stopped working, just after midnight, she'd taken a hot shower to ease her tired muscles, and had gone to bed. When she'd tried to sleep, all she had been able to do was think of Darren, and what she had to say to him—and how she would say it.

Her vacillating emotions and the mind-shattering battle she'd fought had been unresolved by the time she'd fallen asleep. She was certain that both her career and her life itself were at stake. She loved Darren and knew she could not postpone telling him why she was here, not if she wanted their relationship to grow. At the same time, the paradox was all too strong.

If she told him about the valley, she would be breaking her company's trust, and conceivably jeopardizing the project and the millions of dollars invested in it.

Lea also believed that she had an obligation to herself, as well as to Darren. *I must make him understand how important he, as well as the project, is to me.* Lea had worked hard for too many years to give up her dreams at this point.

Why can't I have both? Even at this thought, she once again searched for and found her determination to meet this problem and solve it.

Shaking her head, Lea went back to the closet and surveyed what was left of her wardrobe. Finally, she took down a pair of black jeans and slipped them on. Then she went to the dresser and chose a pale blue knit pullover. After tucking the shirt into her jeans, and putting on a belt, Lea stepped into a pair of flat-heeled loafers.

When she looked at herself again in the mirror, she realized that she looked and felt comfortable.

"I'm ready," she told her reflection. *Maybe,* her mind whispered, challenging her sudden bravado.

Twenty minutes after driving away from the hotel, Lea turned onto the gravel drive leading to Darren's house. Once again, her nerves were stretched so tautly that she could hardly think. Trepidation filled her mind. Anxiety sent a new flash of fear coursing through her.

He will understand, she told herself. *I love him, and he will understand!* Lea followed the gently curved upgrade of the drive, and, as her adamant thoughts faded, she regained some of her confidence.

Just as she pulled the car to a stop next to Darren's Land Rover, she saw him emerge from his studio, a large sketch pad under his arm.

Darren stopped in mid-stride when he saw Lea step out of her car. A rush of warmth spread through him, and he smiled fully at her.

He liked the way her jeans outlined her hips and legs without being too tight. The pale pullover flattered her skin tones and accented her breasts while showing the slimness of her waist. But it was her face that caught his attention.

Exhaling slowly, Darren started toward her. His eyes swept across her features, drinking in his idea of perfection. Reaching out with his free hand, he caught her around the waist and drew her slowly to him. He kissed Lea deeply, moving his lips slowly on hers and tasting the sweetness of their pliant warmth.

When he released her, he smiled again. "I like surprises like this." Before Lea could react or say anything, he turned, tossed his sketch pad in the Land Rover, and grabbed her hand.

"Come with me!" he commanded, his voice laced with excitement.

Lea, her heart pounding with the aftereffects of the kiss, and of the guilty secret she carried within her, could only stare at him. "Where?" she finally asked as she allowed him to drag her toward the door of the Land Rover.

"You'll see," he stated secretively with the same undertone of excitement.

A few moments later they were at the end of Darren's drive. There, he turned right, and started up toward the higher elevations.

"What's happening?" she asked as the road narrowed into a bumpy mountain path. Darren reached down and pulled a lever near the transmission. An instant later, Lea felt the vehicle lurch slightly.

"Four-wheel drive," he informed her needlessly.

"That's not what I mean. Where are we going? Why?"

"Patience," he said with a smile. Lea studied his face as he negotiated the road. Every few seconds, his eyes would flick upward, searching the sky.

When the road became almost nonexistent, and Darren twisted the steering wheel every few seconds to keep the Land Rover moving, Lea quickly buckled her seat belt and grabbed the sides of the seat.

Fifteen minutes later, Darren stopped the Land Rover on a narrow plateau near the mountain's top. Lea's relieved sigh echoed in the confines of the vehicle. Carefully, she unclasped her hands from the edge of the seat and turned to Darren. "The only thing that's ever come close to this ride was the Loch Ness Monster at Busch Gardens."

Darren laughed out loud as he leaned toward her and brushed his lips across her cheek. "This was relatively easy compared to some of the other places I've taken this car."

Smiling secretively again, Darren reached in front of Lea, opened a compartment in the dash, and took out a binocular case. Leaning into the back seat, he picked up his sketch pad and left the vehicle. "Coming?" he asked Lea, who had still not unfastened her seat belt.

"Where?" she asked again. Darren shook his head and started walking away.

Moving quickly, Lea unbuckled the belt, got out of the Land Rover, and half ran to catch up with him, thankful that she'd chosen this outfit, and not one of the dresses.

When she caught up to him, he took her hand in his and silently continued on. As they approached the edge of the plateau, Darren guided them to an outcrop of rocks and, releasing her hand, sat down.

"Sit next to me," he said as he opened the sketch pad and withdrew a piece of charcoal and pencil from his shirt pocket. After placing the pad and sketching implements next to him, he looked at Lea for a moment, and then up at the sky.

Lea, realizing that he was still not ready to tell her what was happening, glanced around for the first time. Above and behind them, the mountain continued to rise for at least another thousand feet. Its peak still held a few random patches of snow left over from winter.

When Lea turned from the peak and looked outward, her breath caught at the magnificence of the scene. They were so high above the rest of the world that she could see for miles. The Sangre de Cristo Mountains' relentless peaks stretched forever and their power and might filled Lea with wonder.

Turning her head slightly, she was even able to view a small part of Stetman's valley from her vantage point. Although Santa Fe itself, ten or so miles away, was blocked by the mountains surrounding it, she knew exactly where it was.

She looked at Darren, who was still staring up at the cloudless sky. "I really do like being alone with you, Darren, but you don't seem to be with me right now....What are we doing?" she finally asked.

Darren held back his smile when he looked at her. "Waiting." Then he looked skyward again.

Lea sighed, and then she, too, started looking up for whatever it was that Darren was hoping to see.

"An hour ago, I saw an eagle flying. If it's the same one I've seen before, this area is part of its hunting grounds. I wanted to watch it."

Lea shook her head helplessly. Then she turned to look at Darren's intensely set face. *Talk to him now,* she ordered herself, realizing that this would be the perfect time.

"Darren," she began hesitantly, her hands locked tightly together.

Darren's hand rose suddenly, cutting her off. Then he stretched out his arm, pointing skyward. "There," he whispered.

In the far distance, Lea saw a dark speck flying toward them. "How do you know it's an eagle?"

"Wait," he said as he picked up his sketch pad and pencil.

The bird grew larger. Within minutes, she could see it clearly. Its graceful flight was accented by slow dips and wide arcs that carried it wherever it wanted to go.

The only eagles she had ever seen were in zoos, or in pictures. None of those had ever prepared her for this sight, or for the size of this particular bird. When it spread its wings to coast on an updraft, her mouth opened in wonder.

Lea felt something being put in her hands. Glancing down, she found Darren's binoculars resting in her palms. Lifting the heavy glasses, she put them to her eyes. After adjusting the focus, she searched the sky until she found the eagle.

Her gasp was loud and explosive. The bird was soaring on another updraft, and its wings were spread wide. In that instant, Lea realized just how large and majestic the giant bird was. Its wingspan had to be at least six feet across.

She saw the tawny feathers on the back of its head and neck, which reflected the sunlight with a golden hue. "He's...I can't describe it," she whispered in awe.

"She," Darren corrected. "Female golden eagles are larger than males." Darren paused for a moment as a smile stole across his lips. "And I can't describe her either...in words," he added as his hand flew over the paper, guiding the pencil without ever taking his eyes from the bird.

Knowing that Darren needed silence to concentrate, Lea held back her next question and lowered the binoculars. Leaning back, she watched the golden eagle.

The giant bird flew proudly, the queen of the sky. It would swoop gracefully toward the earth far below, only to pull up from its steep dive, and circle lazily upward until it reached the same heights it had originally descended from.

After what seemed an eternity, the graceful eagle stopped circling the area and rose even higher. Slowly, the majestic bird began to fade from sight.

Sighing, Darren put down the sketch pad and closed his eyes for a second. When he opened them, he looked at Lea. "Was the trip worth it?" he asked.

Lea nodded.

"Have you ever seen anything like that before?"

Lea shook her head slowly. Reality was returning, and her nerves were tensing again. "How did you know she would be here? Does she live in these mountains?"

"I don't think so," Darren said as he looked up at where the eagle had disappeared. "Civilization has chased the eagles from this area. Most of them live deep in the Rockies. But they have to fly far from home in search of prey."

"She was magnificent," Lea said. "This whole area is magnificent."

"That's why I can't leave here for too long. I would miss the beauty of life that abounds here, the freedom the animals show me. I just pray that nothing will ever change this."

"Why should it?" Lea asked, her voice low.

Darren stared deeply at her, his eyes reflecting the intensity of his inner self. "People are always trying to change things. To 'improve' the land, so they say." Darren fell silent for a moment, his eyes no less probing than before.

"I've just learned that some company has bought Stetman's valley." His arm swept outward until his index finger was pointing toward the distant valley. "I met you in Stetman's valley. We're sure they're going to build a development of some sort there."

"*We're* sure?" Lea asked hesitantly.

"I'm a member of a group dedicated to protecting the land in New Mexico—the Environmental Preservation League."

Lea stared at him and foresaw the destruction of what they might have been to each other. *How can I tell him now?* Suddenly Lea realized that her thought no longer held any validity; the truth of the matter was that he had just voiced his prejudice against her project, and against her as well. With his one statement, he had thrown a solid barrier between them. *What can I do?*

Fight, she commanded herself. *Fight for him. Make him see what you see!*

Slowly, battling against the wave of sadness that was enveloping her, Lea moistened her lips. "Not all land development is bad. There are designs and methods that could even improve the areas they use." After speaking, she tried to see what effects her words had on him, but she saw no change on his stiffly set features.

"I seriously doubt that!" Raising his hand, he placed it lightly on Lea's shoulder. "Besides, that's the architect in you speaking."

Lea wasn't quite sure if he meant to be as patronizing as his words had sounded. Holding back her threatening anger, she took a deep breath before responding. "Is it?" Lea asked. "How do you know that it's not the woman in the architect rather than the other way around?"

"Because of how I feel about you."

Lea froze. She stared at him silently, trapped by despair. "Why do you think a small development in this area would necessarily disrupt or destroy everything?"

"Because it interrupts the life cycle."

"Not always. Darren, I know how you feel about the land, but there must be a way that people and nature can live together."

"They can't," he repeated stubbornly, his voice filled with his own confidence in the rightness of his cause.

"But *you* do! How can you say that others can't live here, too, without harming their surroundings?" she challenged.

"We're not talking about a single dwelling, or even several houses spread out in the mountains. We're talking about an entire community, and the significance of what that means to the valley in terms of construction and long-term degeneration of the land."

"Humor me for a moment," Lea asked, her expression as serious as Darren's. When Darren nodded, Lea continued. "A small community, utilizing the land, building upon it without destroying or tearing it down, is feasible."

"Perhaps."

Lea ignored this. "It is; I know that for a fact. If the work, the construction, is done carefully, the wildlife in the area will be disturbed for only a short period. The wildlife will eventually return to their natural patterns without any harm."

"I didn't know you were a biologist as well as an ecologist," Darren said in a tight voice.

"I guess you do now," Lea retorted sharply. A moment later she reined in her surging emotions. "Darren, I don't want to argue with you."

Darren searched her face. "I get carried away sometimes. But I've seen what happens when people take unspoiled land and change it to suit themselves. The evidence is all around us, wherever we go." Darren paused for a moment, thinking of a hundred different examples. He wanted to explain himself to Lea, to make her understand what drove him to protect what was left of the country.

"The government chose the desert to test atomic weapons because it supposedly would not affect mankind. But they were wrong. Although those tests ended twenty years ago, the effects are still with us. They destroyed wildlife and land in their shortsighted, unthinking way, and the aftereffects hurt mankind."

"Building a community for people is not bombing the land."

"It is, in a different way."

"Darren, since I've met you, I've never thought that you were a closed-minded person. I never expected you to be the type of man who made irrational judgments."

"I'm not," Darren said in a level voice. "I have the knowledge to make my judgments. I've seen people move into virgin areas. I've watched them change the environment and turn beauty into a pile of prefabricated structures and fast-food restaurants!"

"So have I," Lea stated, her mind vacillating between her own belief in what she was doing and Darren's one-sided view. "But what if the people who come to Stetman's valley don't change things? What if they're people who love nature. People who use it properly instead of abusing it?"

"There ain't no such animal," Darren snapped angrily. His entire body had stiffened at Lea's argument, and he could not help his harsh response.

"I think there is," Lea whispered in counterpoint. "You're surrounded by beauty, Darren, but you're selfish. You don't want to share it with others."

Suddenly Darren laughed. "But I do. With every brushstroke I take, I share it."

Lea nodded. "Yes, you're sharing your own particular view of what you see. Other people may see the same thing differently. To older people, retired men and women who've spent their lives working and living in a city, this would look one way; to the younger generations, to children, it would be seen through vastly different eyes."

"Which is what makes the world so nice," Darren said, lightening the mood. "Lea, I can't help the way I feel. I just know it would be wrong to ruin a place like Stetman's valley.''

Darren turned from her and picked up the sketching pad. He looked at what he'd done, and then handed it to Lea.

Leas stared at the penciled lines' image of the eagle. She could see, in the half-formed, uncolored strokes, the might and strength of the giant bird.

Then she glanced up at Darren. A strong and sudden wave of emotion washed over her, and her heart fluttered as she handed the pad back to him. Their fingers brushed, and heat spread quickly through her hand. *I love you*, she told him silently.

Darren and Lea spent another hour on the high mountain plateau. While Darren worked on his sketch with charcoal this time, Lea wandered around, looking everywhere but seeing nothing.

Her eyes continually turned back to Darren. Her dark thoughts swirled tortuously, centering upon her predicament. *He was the enemy!* she told herself. Darren was the very obstacle standing in the path of her dreams.

Her mind was filled with doubt while she tried to figure out if she should speak to Darren about who she was, and why she was there. But the more she thought, the more certain she became that Darren's own prejudices would rise up between them.

If I tell him, it will be over for us. If I tell him, he will know whom to fight, and I will lose everything—my career and my love. But I have to try, no matter what the risk.

Twice, as Darren worked and Lea stood nearby watching him, she tried to find the willpower to speak

You know the thrill of
escaping to a world where
Love, Romance, and
Happiness reach out
to one and all...

Escape again...with 4 FREE novels and

get more great Silhouette Special Edition novels —for a 15-day FREE examination— delivered to your door every month!

Silhouette Special Edition novels are written especially for you, someone who knows the allure, the enchantment and the power of romance. Romance *is* alive, and flourishing in these moving love stories that let you escape to exotic places with sensitive heroines and captivating men.

Written by such popular authors as Janet Dailey, Donna Vitek, Diana Dixon, and others, Silhouette Special Edition novels help you reach that special world—month after month. They'll take you to that world you have always imagined, where you will live and breathe the emotions of love and the satisfaction of romance triumphant.

FREE BOOKS

Start today by taking advantage of this special offer— 4 new Silhouette Special Edition romances (a $10.00 Value) *absolutely FREE,* along with a Cameo Tote Bag. Just fill out and mail the attached postage-paid order card.

AT-HOME PREVIEWS, FREE DELIVERY

After you receive your 4 free books and Tote Bag, every month you'll have the opportunity to preview 6 more Silhouette Special Edition romances— *as soon as they're published!* When you decide to keep them, you'll pay just $11.70, (a $15.00 value), *with never an additional charge of any kind and no risk!* You can cancel your subscription at any time simply by dropping us a note. In any case, the first 4 books, and Cameo Tote Bag are yours to keep.

EXTRA BONUS

When you take advantage of this offer, we'll also send you the Silhouette Books Newsletter free with each shipment. Every informative issue features news about upcoming titles, interviews with your favorite authors, and even their favorite recipes.

Get a Free
Tote Bag, too!

**EVERY BOOK YOU RECEIVE WILL BE
A BRAND-NEW FULL-LENGTH NOVEL!**

Escape with 4 Silhouette Special Edition novels (a $10.00 Value) and get a FREE Tote Bag, too!

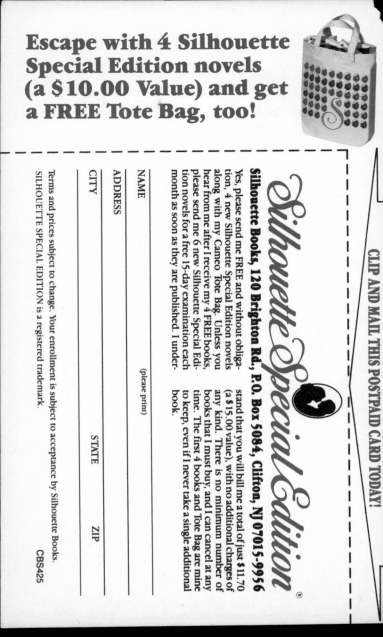

Silhouette Special Edition ®

Silhouette Books, 120 Brighton Rd., P.O. Box 5084, Clifton, NJ 07015-9956

Yes, please send me FREE and without obligation, 4 new Silhouette Special Edition novels along with my Cameo Tote Bag. Unless you hear from me after I receive my 4 FREE books, please send me 6 new Silhouette Special Edition novels for a free 15-day examination each month as soon as they are published. I understand that you will bill me a total of just $11.70 (a $15.00 value), with no additional charges of any kind. There is no minimum number of books that I must buy, and I can cancel at any time. The first 4 books and Tote Bag are mine to keep, even if I never take a single additional book.

NAME _____
(please print)

ADDRESS _____

CITY _____ STATE _____ ZIP _____

Terms and prices subject to change. Your enrollment is subject to acceptance by Silhouette Books.
SILHOUETTE SPECIAL EDITION is a registered trademark.

CBS425

to him. But his concentration was so totally fixed on his work that she realized he hadn't heard her feeble attempts at confession.

Finally, as her nerves were once again reaching the breaking point, Darren finished.

When they started to drive back, Darren, belatedly aware of how the ride up the mountain had affected Lea, drove back to his house slowly.

Once there, they had a light lunch on the deck. But the mood created by the eagle was gone, and the lingering effects of the argument still bothered him.

Gazing at Lea, who was looking up again at the mountain's peak, he saw the telltale lines of tension around her mouth and believed she was still upset. "About before," Darren said abruptly.

Lea turned to Darren. Arching her eyebrows, she waited for him to continue.

"I didn't mean to get so argumentative before. It's just that I'm totally committed to ecology."

"It's all right. You wouldn't be who you are if you didn't care so deeply." *Now! Tell him now before you can't tell him at all. Make him understand*, she cried to herself.

Darren smiled at her. In that very moment, he realized that he could no longer hold to himself what he knew he must tell her. He saw that Lea was about to say something, but he spoke first. His voice was low.

"I love you, Lea. But you know that already, don't you?"

Lea stared at him, her eyes misting and turning his face into a filmy vision. She tried to speak but failed. Then her tears spilled out from her eyes and trailed downward along her cheeks. Her mouth suddenly tasted moist and salty.

Slowly, Lea nodded. "I love you, Darren, and I think you knew that before I did."

Darren left his chair and drew Lea to her feet. He held her to him, and carefully wiped the tears from her eyes. Then he bent and tenderly kissed her lips.

When they parted, their eyes glowed. But then the sobering realization of the future again intruded on Lea's happiness. "Darren, we're so different. We believe in different things...."

"Do we? I'm not so sure."

"What happened on the mountain is an example. We were arguing, and it wasn't pretty."

"We were expressing opinions," Darren countered.

"But what I do for a living is against all your ideals."

"Is it?"

"I...I'm afraid that it could be," Lea admitted, her voice again tight. "I'm an architect and a designer. I build communities where there are none. I'm the person you have to hate."

"No," Darren said quickly. "I will never hate you." Then he took a deep breath and shook his head. "Enough!" he declared. "No more arguments. Today is only for us, and nothing else."

"Darren," Lea protested, not wanting to be stopped from her admission.

"Lea, no more." This time his words were softer, and accented by his hands as they cupped her face. His lips covered hers, and under their sweet and fiery assault, her determination to tell him the truth was abandoned once again.

The rest of the day flew by in a whirlwind of activity as Darren once again played guide to Lea's wide-eyed tourist's fascination with the countryside, and the natural and manmade wonders.

They talked of the natural beauty that was spread out like a banquet for their hungry eyes. As Darren pointed out several unusually colorful rock formations, he contrasted the way nature gave freely of its bounty to the way man took it and changed it.

But those diatribes never lasted for too long. Lea found herself in agreement for the most part with Darren's opinions as to the manner in which most people stole from nature rather than utilizing her offerings without destroying them.

Fortunately, the sightseeing tour provided more reasons for enjoying the day, and less for arguing about man's encroachment upon the remaining free lands.

Their last stop of the day was at Echo Amphitheater, a cliffside eroded by time into a natural cavity, which had a truly remarkable acoustic quality that magnified a voice into an eerie echo.

By late afternoon, when they took off from the amphitheater, the once clear and blue sky had filled with clouds, and the warm, late-spring afternoon had turned unseasonably chilly.

An hour and a half after leaving the amphitheater, they were back at Darren's house. The day had already ended, and the sunset had been invisible behind the cloud-shrouded sky. Inside, Darren piled logs in the large stone fireplace.

Once again, they prepared dinner together and ate informally at the kitchen table. After dinner, Darren lit the fire and Lea brought the bottle of wine they'd opened, along with their glasses.

When the fire had grown to the right size and the chill in the air was gone, Darren and Lea kicked off their shoes and relaxed on the woven Indian blanket in front of the fire place.

A comfortable silence—broken only by the snap of burning wood—the light scent of pine smoke, and the gentle background sounds of the stereo hovered around the two of them. With Darren's arm around her shoulder, Lea sipped from her wineglass and then rested her head against him.

The orange flames licked upward in the fireplace; the crackling of the fire was a gentle counterpoint to the beating of her heart. Yet, as relaxed as her body was, and as secure as she felt within Darren's hold, her mind would not be still, and her thoughts continued to haunt her.

Lea tried to accept the situation. She had never deceived Darren intentionally, and even when she'd learned how much of a threat he represented to her professional life, she had decided to trust her heart and speak to him truthfully. But each time she'd tried to tell him about herself, he'd stopped her.

Their argument on the mountain was a vivid reminder that what she had to tell Darren would not be easy. His thoughts and feelings about land development were very strong, and totally biased, although in some respects he had been right. Lea could only pray that the love they had finally admitted to each other could be the one thing that held them together, despite their differences.

Turning slightly, Lea gazed at the handsome profile so near to her. She drank in the angular lines of his face, and the soft curve of his short beard. When he had been espousing his beliefs earlier, she had seen an immovable hardness settle on his features. *Would that too return with her confession?*

Taking a deep, preparatory breath, Lea reached up and covered his hand with hers, pressing his palm firmly onto her shoulder. "Darren, I need to talk to you."

Darren exerted pressure on her shoulder and looked at her. "Talk," he whispered.

"It's about me," she began, her tone level but words hesitant, "and about my work."

"I know everything I need to know about you, Lea. I know that I love you, and that I trust you." Darren paused. He placed his glass on the floor, and turned more fully to her. Bending his head, he kissed her gently. "Do you remember the other day at the valley, and what I said?"

Lea stared at him, her mouth suddenly dry.

"I said that we don't need any explanations between us. That the past is no longer a part of our world. I still feel the same way."

Will you feel this way later? is what she wanted to ask; but the words would not come. Instead, tears built up behind her eyes and slowly spilled out. She had just discovered the answer to all her silent questions. She knew now, without a doubt, that when she told him the truth about herself he would no longer feel the same way toward her.

The revelation had been apparent in his attitude. In his effort to calm her whirling emotions, he had said things that terrified her and told her the folly of her situation. "Trust" was what he had said. Would he ever trust her again after she revealed her secret?

Darren stared at Lea, and when he saw her tears, a lump lodged in his throat. "What's wrong?" he asked, his voice a husky whisper.

"Nothing...everything," she confessed at the realization that she had been fooling herself. She instinctively knew that when she told him the truth, he would react exactly as he had on the mountain, if not worse. She couldn't tell him, not now.

"Lea?"

"Please, Darren, don't ask, just hold me."

Darren put his other arm around her and drew her close, pulling her tightly to him and holding her safely within his arms. After a few more silent seconds, he felt her stir, and, looking down at her tear-streaked face, he bent and kissed her.

What had started as a gentle kiss soon turned into an all-consuming act of giving, and, as their breathing deepened, the kiss grew longer. When Darren's mouth finally left hers, she gazed up at him. His features were illuminated by the dancing flames.

The loss that would soon be hers, doomed by her secrecy, made her speak out of despair, need, and love.

"Love me, Darren. Please make love to me."

Chapter Eight

The magic of Darren's touch chased the specter of foreboding and disaster. Lea's pulse quickened and her breathing was shaky.

The fire burning in the background and the music floating in the air above them helped to release her from her desperate thoughts, and allowed her to believe that she and Darren would always be together.

The fingers that had held the pencil and charcoal that morning now traced the outlines of Lea's body. Their mouths came together; Lea tasted the warmth of his lips. Her body pressed closer to his, and her blood raced swiftly.

Her breathing quickened as his lips pressed to hers, and deep within her, flames roared into life and spread through her. She was helpless, under the assault of her own sad thoughts and his heated passionate caresses, to do anything except be held and kissed by him.

Her body would not move. Her hands refused to obey her command to caress his strong back. The desperate hopelessness that overshadowed her thoughts and controlled her passion gave vent to her deep need to be held and kissed and loved by Darren.

Without taking his lips from hers, Darren shifted, slowly lowering their bodies to the blanket. His blood was pulsing strongly through his body, and all too soon, his desire threatened to take full control of his actions. In a swirling instant, Darren fought for and won control over his passion.

Lea drifted from reality. Although she knew she was safe within Darren's arms, she forced her eyes open to look at him. She used his face as an anchor to hold back her rushing emotions and stop them from robbing her of this moment.

Taking her arms from around him, she reached for his face. Her hands captured his cheeks and drew him to her; his beard tickled the sensitive skin on her palms. Their lips met in a kiss so soft and gentle that it bespoke much more than just passion.

When Darren took his mouth from hers, Lea could not stop her small cry of protest. Then his lips traced over her closed eyelids. With every slow movement they made, a tingling reverberated in her stomach.

His lips roamed her face, tasting and kissing every inch of skin until his mouth rejoined hers. The kiss deepened, and whatever unreleased passions still lay beneath Darren's surface rushed outward.

Lea's arms returned to his back, her hands pressing tightly, rubbing and caressing the rippling muscles through the thin cotton of his shirt.

Their tongues joined in a dance of love. Their bodies were pressed tightly against each other. Darren's powerful chest covered her breasts, and his strong thighs lay upon hers. Her mind spun as she lost herself to the kiss, and to the feel of the man she loved.

Once again Darren drew his mouth from hers. Lea stiffened, her hands turning into claws, trying vainly to hold him to her. But he slipped away.

She saw a shadowy smile curving his lips while his eyes caressed her face. An instant later his lips were on the sensitive skin at the base of her throat, and as they burned against her, she released a low moan of pleasure.

His mouth was maddening as it kissed every sensitive place on her neck, and then suddenly, his hand was cupping her breast. Her back arched when the heat of his hand set her breast aflame.

Her right hand moved, tracing the outline of his neck, even as her left hand trailed along the small of his back, her fingertips racing across the fabric of his shirt.

Again Darren pulled away. He stared down at her, his body tense with desire. When he saw her gazing back at him, her large eyes open and filled with love, he knew that his love had been given to the right woman. Carefully, Darren began to unbutton her top.

The seconds flew by while Darren slowly undressed Lea. With each piece of clothing he removed, he stopped to look upon her beauty, to kiss and caress her before continuing on.

When her pale blue top was gone, Darren held his breath as he gazed at the perfection of her breasts. Her skin was silken smooth, an alabaster surface. Bending, he caressed first one breast and then the other, before taking the stiffened tips within his mouth.

Lea, her head tossed back, her eyes closed, let the pleasure of his touch fill her. The pulsating sensations emanating from her breasts increased with each caress. And when his mouth captured her nipple, she cried out unknowingly.

Then he was undoing her belt and, as he slid her pants down, he stopped every few inches to let his hand caress the inside of her velvety thighs; all the while, he was unable to take his eyes from the incredible beauty of her form.

He paused to drink in the glowing surface of her naked body, a sight he knew he would never grow tired of seeing. "You are too beautiful to be real," he told her in a husky voice.

Lea's eyes misted for a moment as his words reminded her of all that had happened in the past few days. "I am real, my love," she whispered in a faraway voice. *Too real, perhaps*, she added to herself.

Darren stood, looking down at her for a long moment. "I know." Then he undressed.

For Lea, the next few minutes created a memory that would remain with her for the rest of her life. Darren was framed by the fireplace, and the ethereal glow of the fire seemed to become a part of him.

Lea watched the interplay of his stomach muscles, and the forced rise and fall of his chest. Then his pants were gone, and she couldn't stop herself from drinking in every part of his body.

When Darren started to lower himself toward her, she raised her arms in a silent call to him. Slowly, he knelt and joined her on the blanket.

Their mouths came together in a wildly passionate kiss as their hands roamed freely, exploring each other's bodies. The flames within her grew stronger and rose like a tidal wave on the open sea. Lea had no choice but to let herself flow with it.

Then they were on their sides, and her hand glided along his skin until it reached the curve of his hip. Her other hand was enmeshed in his hair; her breasts were crushed by his chest. His hands traced a maddening pathway along her sides. A tingling heat radiated from wherever he touched her. A moment later Darren drew his lips from hers and turned her onto her back.

Staring down at her, looking into her large, dewy eyes, Darren smiled gently. Then he lowered himself along her length. His hands captured her full breasts, caressing them lightly at first, but more firmly as his passion built.

He lavished each breast with equal care and love, until he heard Lea crying out with the pleasure he strove to give her. Refusing to heed her cries, he lowered himself and tasted the silk of her abdomen. His mouth roamed everywhere, kissing and caressing until Lea's back arched and her fingernails dug into his shoulders.

Lea's body trembled with each kiss and caress. She was in the grip of a fever that could only be quenched by Darren. But, no matter how she called to him or urged him to her, he would not listen, and finally, Lea couldn't fight him.

Darren shifted again and his hand, gentle but insistent, wandered through the downy hair before dipping lower to caress the trembling skin of her inner thighs. A moment later his hand returned to the entrance of her womanhood. Sparks flew before her eyes; a vein in her neck pulsed with every wild beat of her heart.

Her hands found his hair again and weaved within the dark mass. Her mind swam dizzily, and she bit down on her lower lip, ignoring the pain.

Shimmering lances of firelight, reflected on the ceiling of the living room, bounced madly in her eyes as a rolling wave of desire ebbed and flowed through her with his never-ending caresses.

Then his touch was gone. Lea cried out, but before her cry had faded, Darren's lips were on hers, his body poised above her. When he lowered himself upon her, she gasped.

Her eyes opened wide, and she stared into Darren's blue depths. Lea banished the sadness and loss that were still so much a part of her, and allowed herself to believe, for this one special moment in time, that there was nothing to fear. Later, everything would be all right.

Darren moved slowly, entering her with a gentleness that defied his daring passions. He kissed her deeply, and felt her body open to his in complete acceptance.

When they were one again, Lea tore her lips from his, burying her mouth in the joining of his neck and shoulder as her arms tightened around Darren's muscular torso, holding on to him as if she could keep him with her forever.

"I love you," she whispered, her voice breaking beneath the intensity of her emotions.

Suddenly everything changed. Lea could not feel the blanket beneath her, or the heat from the fire on her skin. Her world had shifted, and only she and Darren existed, joined together by their love.

Their entwined bodies moved as one, and with every gentle thrust of Darren's hips, Lea returned the same. Their hands caressed, explored, and learned, while their bodies ascended upward, climbing the triple peaks of love, passion, and desire.

They stayed locked together for an eternity, touching, holding, loving, and blending together in a pattern as old as time itself, yet as new as each discovery of their love.

Without warning, Lea's body tensed. Her back arched and her eyes flew open. Wave after wave of the most incredible sensations flowed through her, sending lances of pleasure to every part of her body. She cried out Darren's name, even as she felt him stiffen. Together they reached the pinnacle of their lovemaking.

Lea, her breathing raspy in the air, her arms clasped tightly around Darren, could feel his heart pound against her breasts. She willed herself to luxuriate in his warm breath across her cheek for as long as was humanly possible.

While she was being held so closely by Darren, she made herself remember everything that had happened since the first day they'd met, strengthening her memories so that she would never forget him, or the love that they had shared.

For Lea, as she gazed at the sleeping form of Darren, the entire night seemed to be dimmed by a misty haze that grew clearer instead of foggier.

After their intensely beautiful lovemaking, they had lain together on the Indian blanket for hours, neither saying very much, both watching the flames in the fire-place and feeling their closeness.

When the fire had been replaced by softly glowing embers, and the chill of the damp night outside invaded the air, Darren had stood and drawn Lea to her feet. He'd taken her upstairs to his bedroom, where they had once again made love before falling asleep in each other's arms.

Lea closed her eyes for a moment. When she opened them, she looked at Darren's handsome, peaceful face. Her eyes wandered freely, taking in the broad expanse of his smoothly rising and falling chest. The pattern of dark hair on it was yet another memory she wanted to remember forever.

In sleep, Darren's face was no less handsome than when he was awake. The same strong lines dominated the planes of his face; only the radiating pattern of his smile lines at the corners of his eyes were gone.

Tears suddenly veiled her sight as she looked at him and remembered his words of love and trust. They shook her, for she did love him deeply.

Why did it happen like this? she asked herself. But Lea knew there was no answer for her. Life had its own mysteries, and love was one of them.

As she gazed at him in the darkened bedroom, she could again feel the power of his arms around her, a feeling she was sure she would never know again. "I love you," she whispered, her voice no louder than Darren's own even breathing. "Good-bye."

With a heavy rush of irrevocable loss, Lea left the bed, moving carefully so as not to disturb Darren.

A few moments later, she was dressed and sitting at the kitchen table, the pen in her hand hovering above the blank paper.

Finally, she steeled herself to write; she refused to let the tears falling on the paper stop her from her obligation.

When the note was finished, Lea took a deep, trembling breath and stood. Picking up her purse, she shut off the kitchen light and left the house.

Outside, Lea glanced up at the moonless, cloud-filled night. Shuddering, not with the chill but because of her own emotions, she went to the car and started it. Before she could leave, a strange and twisting moment out of time seemed to wrench Lea.

Suddenly she was seeing her mother standing at her drafting table: Janice Graham's face was set in intent lines as she listened to a sixteen-year-old Lea tell her that she was going to be an architect just like her mother.

"It isn't an easy life, Lea."

"But you're doing it. You have your career, and you have me and father."

"You can have a career and a family, but you must be willing to accept the sacrifices involved in having both. A halfhearted attempt with either will only bring unhappiness."

Opening her eyes, Lea dismissed the vision that this emotionally devastating night had conjured. A moment later she felt the solidity of the steering wheel beneath her hands and heaved a sigh of relief. As she drove away, the dashboard clock informed her that the new day would be coming all too soon.

Darren woke slowly as the sun filtered in through the large bedroom window. Stretching without opening his eyes, he reached for Lea. When his hands found only emptiness, he sat up quickly and looked around, but Lea was nowhere to be seen.

Tossing the cover from him, Darren left the bed, slipped on a pair of jeans, and started from the room. He was conscious that he'd slept much later than usual and when he reached the foot of the stairs, he looked at the old grandfather clock in the downstairs hallway, noting that it was almost nine o'clock.

"Lea," he called. He peered into the living room, but she was not there. When he entered the kitchen, and found it empty, he was puzzled. Then his eyes fell on the kitchen table, and he saw the note.

He went to the table, sat and started reading. When he finished, his body was stiff; the muscles in his neck were knotted.

Slowly, trying to understand what was happening, Darren reread the note.

Dear Darren,

This is the most difficult thing I have ever had to do. I love you so deeply that every time I think of just how much I do, I begin to cry inside. I have never before felt the emotions that you have brought out in me, and never expect to again.

These past few days have been the happiest of my life, and I can only hope that I've made you feel the same way. But, life has a way of taking that which one wants and loves the most, and yesterday I realized just how true that is, and how cruel life can be.

I can only hope and pray that, in time, you will understand why I had to do this. I want to ask for your forgiveness, though I don't believe you will be able to forgive me. Yet I will hope that the love we shared will not be forgotten, and your love not replaced with anger.

I love you,
Lea.

"Why, Lea?" Darren asked aloud. Then he suddenly balled the note in his hand and flung it from him. Standing, he turned, went back to the bedroom, and dressed. Ten minutes after reading Lea's note, he was in his Land Rover, heading for Santa Fe.

Lea paced nervously in the arrivals area of Albuquerque's International Airport, waiting for Robert Kanter to debark. He had come in on the nine-fifteen flight, but it had been delayed a half hour.

Lea glanced at the electronic sign and, seeing the flight number flashing, knew the plane was finally on the ground. *And so it begins,* Lea said silently. She thought of the old saying that "today is the first day of the rest of your life," but shrugged it off.

She had committed herself to her career goals long before reaching college, and since then had worked hard to achieve them. She had made a commitment to the valley project, and had already given two years of her life to that.

Her loyalty had been hard tested, and it was still divided. But within her, there was a grim determination to maintain self-respect. If Darren was not so violently opposed to change, things might have been different. But he was. To have told him of her work, knowing how much he opposed her work and the project, would have been a violation of her personal as well as professional ethics. It would have become another issue standing between them.

Lea had finally understood this last night. But she had not been strong enough to just leave Darren. Her love and desire for him had kept her secret locked within her, while she held Darren to her, and loved him one final time.

She knew that last deception was the worst of all, and that she should be ashamed. She *was* ashamed, but she was also glad that she and Darren had made love one last time. She had needed to feel his arms about her, to have him within her; it was a memory that she would carry with her forever.

She pleaded with herself to think of something, anything else, as her eyes misted again. When she saw the line of passengers approaching the gate, she summoned her strength to replace the weakness of her heart.

By the time Robert reached her, she had gained a modicum of control over her emotions and greeted her boss with a smile.

"Good flight?"

"Good enough," he replied, shifting the overnight bag to his other shoulder. "How are we doing?" he asked as they started toward the exit.

"Good. I brought all the fact sheets with me, and everything is prepared to set up for filing. Do you want to go to the hotel first, or to the valley?"

"The valley," Robert said.

After retrieving the car, and while paying the parking fee, Lea opened her attaché case and handed Robert her paperwork. While she drove, she glanced occasionally at him as he looked over the work.

Because of unusually heavy traffic, the trip back to Santa Fe took almost an hour and a half. Twenty minutes after that, Lea pulled the car to a stop at the mouth of Stetman's valley.

Shutting the engine off, she turned to look at Robert, her nerves taut while she waited to find out whether the culmination of two long, hard years of work would be approved, or thrown in the garbage.

A few moments later, Robert looked up from the paperwork, a serious, contemplative expression on his face. "I can't believe you've accomplished so much." Then he shook his head. "You're a marvel," he added.

"It looks okay?"

"It looks better than okay. Of course I'll have to go over it more carefully later, but so far I haven't spotted any problems and it's much better detailed than the last report. Now, let's walk over to the areas where you've made those innovations and see if they'll fit in properly with everything else."

Smiling, Lea led Robert into the valley. As they walked, she let the excitement of what she envisioned propel her words and describe more than what could be built.

"I don't think it's necessary to go to such extremes with the office buildings," Robert suggested. "You have to remember that the residential areas, and even the school and recreation facilities, will be a radical departure for most of the people."

"I haven't forgotten that, Robert. I did the initial behavioral study. But after realizing that we may have a fight on our hands with the ecology group, I thought that by extending the basic plan to cover the three buildings that were not originally a part of it, it would help when it came time to really fight them."

"Perhaps, but to me it seems that it could be a little risky."

"Not *could be* risky—it *will be*, but," Lea said, her determined gaze locking with Robert's, "I think it's a chance we have to take."

Robert shook his head slowly. "It's something the board will have to decide. But I'm willing to listen to whatever you have to say about it."

"Thank you," Lea replied. Then she paused to look around. "When are we going to file the papers?" Her body stiffened involuntarily, and her nerves hummed with tension while she awaited his answer.

Behind her, Robert's voice was loud in the quiet valley. "I've brought all the forms with me, and they've been signed by Mr. Lansing. We'll go over your figures later, and then transfer them to the forms. You'll have to do the final submission package, have it bound, and get Randolph Hastings in Albuquerque to sign it. How long will that take?"

"With a good typist, not more than a week."

"We'll file then," Kanter stated.

Nodding, Lea then turned back to Robert. "What about the finished proposed plans and sketches for the State Building Commission, and the Department of Environment? My sketches won't be good enough."

"They won't have to be. Jason Browning is flying out in two days to work with you."

"Good," Lea stated. She had always liked Jason's work, and considered him to be one of the finest architectural renderers in the country.

Jason Browning had started work at Lansing and Mitchell shortly before Lea had. When they had worked together for the first time, Lea had discovered that Jason showed a sensitivity to her ideas, and had been able to transform her rough sketches into remarkable finished artwork.

"It will give you a chance to make any further changes that might be necessary."

Lea nodded in agreement. Then she smiled at him. "Come, I want you to see how I'm planning to blend the school into the hillside."

For another hour, Lea guided Robert along the valley floor, again pointing out the locations she had already charted and drawn, but this time, she explained all of the procedures she wanted to use to ensure that the area's wildlife would not be endangered.

"What about the marketing study and the shopping alternatives?"

Lea glanced around. "Only the necessities should be part of the complex. There must be a supermarket, drug store, hardware and stationery store, plus a few small miscellaneous retail outlets, and a medical facility. No malls. We're only a short drive from Santa Fe, and a mall would of necessity compete with Santa Fe's retailers. That will create more problems, and give the retailers a reason to side with the conservationists.

"Movies and other recreational facilities are nearby. Also," Lea added, "there is a wealth of restaurants and night spots in town. You know that Santa Fe is the Southwest's cultural capital. The people living here won't lack for opera, ballet, or concerts. All we need is a good restaurant for the residents, and,'' she said with a twinkle in her eyes, ''that will be good for those people who live in the area, and want to see what this community is all about.''

''I understand what you're saying, but by cutting back on retail stores and on an entertainment complex, you'll also cut back on profits.''

''Really?'' Lea challenged quickly. ''Or will it stand as an example of modern architecture that will bring more commissions to Lansing and Mitchell, and bring the company's profit-and-loss statement higher into the black each year? Don't let immediate profit interfere with our original purpose.''

Slowly, Robert nodded his head. ''I'll talk to the board about it. Perhaps the public relations aspects will appeal to their future considerations.''

They were standing in the same clearing that Lea had rested in the other day. As Robert looked around again, he commented on her plans. ''I can visualize most of what you've said, Lea, but it's hard to see the overall view without an aerial map. You do have one at the hotel?''

Lea smiled boldly. ''I have something better,'' she stated confidently. Even as she spoke, she thrust aside the disturbing memories as she thought of the special place where she had met Darren, and had made love to him.

After they returned to the car, Lea drove slowly along the dirt road, pointing out different views of interest to Robert. Reaching the crest, and the spot where she had previously parked her car, Lea's heart almost stopped in a fearful anticipation of what she might find. But when she saw that Darren's Land Rover was not in sight, she breathed easier.

A few minutes later, she was pointing out all the locations of the buildings, explaining to Robert how important it was for their construction to utilize the existing terrain in harmony with it.

"You do know," Robert began, after a lull in Lea's commentary, "that more than just the money Lansing and Mitchell has put into this project is at stake?"

"I believe I do," she replied. "The whole of the architectural community will be watching us, looking closely at every move we make. They'll be waiting to see whether we can pull this off or not. If we do, it can conceivably open up new doorways for expansion into areas we've never been allowed to enter."

"There's more," Robert stated.

"Isn't that enough?" Lea asked dryly in a blatant attempt to avoid the one thing she did not want to hear.

"Everyone's attention will be on you. Your future, your career is on the line. If this ecologically designed, intergenerational community is a success, you will be too. If not—"

"If not," Lea interrupted, "I won't have a career. But it will work, Robert," Lea declared emphatically. "It has to. I've given up too much for it to fail."

Robert held Lea's gaze for a minute, until he slowly shrugged his shoulders and smiled at her. "It will work," he told her confidently. "Now, fill me in on some other details," he ordered.

Turning back, he pointed to the high rim surrounding the valley. "I know the drainage survey reports assure us that there will be no problem with snow and spring thaw, but looking at it now, I wonder if it's truly accurate.''

Lea nodded. ''I thought the same thing, but last winter, when I was here...'' Lea began, explaining to Robert about the additional surveys she'd done, along with the on-site inspection report from Randolph Hastings, the architect in Albuquerque who was working with them.

While Lea continued to fill him in on the details concerning the mountain drainage, they walked along the edge of the valley, moving slowly away from where they'd left the car. But, a sudden feeling of being watched invaded Lea's mind.

Turning quickly, she gasped. Her sharply indrawn breath echoed loudly in the air as she stared at Darren, standing not ten yards away. Color drained from her face, and the world spun madly.

Chapter Nine

After arriving at the hotel, Darren had gone to Lea's room and knocked. He'd waited a full minute for her to come to the door, then he'd knocked again.

When there was still no response, Darren had gone to the dining room, but hadn't found Lea there either. Then he'd walked to the front desk to see if they knew where she was.

"Miss Graham left early this morning," the clerk had said, his stony face set in the traditionally impassive lines of hotel desk clerks all over the world, while his gray eyes had scrutinized Darren.

"Do you know when she'll return?"

"She left no word. However," the clerk had added, "she made a reservation for another guest who is arriving today."

"I see," Darren said, even though he didn't understand. "Then she should be back soon?"

The clerk shrugged noncommittally.

Who can this person be? Darren wondered. A dark and unsettling thought dampened his spirits. The tone of her note should have been the tip-off. "What name is the reservation under?" he asked.

The clerk raised his eyebrows at this question, but remained silent.

Darren's eyes clouded; his hands became tight balls hanging at his side. "It's important," he told the clerk.

"It's highly unusual..."

Darren reached into his pocket and withdrew his money, causing the clerk to wave his hand in dismissal of Darren's action. "Please, Mr. Laird, that's unnecessary."

"You know who I am?"

"Of course. I've seen your work many times." The clerk, his features relaxing, looked down at the cards on the countertop. "Well, you're not really a stranger. Miss Graham reserved the room for a Mr. Robert Kanter."

"Thank you," Darren whispered, the harsh fact that it was a man who was meeting Lea hitting him full force. Absently, he turned from the desk and strode to one of the couches in the lobby. Sitting, he did his best to organize his thoughts.

Anger, jealousy, and loss seethed inside him, robbing him of his ability to think clearly. *Is it because of this man?* he wondered. *Has she been using me to while away her time until this man came? What other reason could there be?* he asked himself.

Darren knew he would have to find out. He was unwilling to accept the evidence that Lea had used him as a passing affair. His love for her would not permit that. Never a man to shy away from confrontation, he decided to wait until Lea returned.

Whatever the reason for her note, he wanted to hear it from her own lips, not rely on a tearstained piece of paper. But after waiting for almost two hours, Darren could no longer sit still under the ruthless and continual bombardment of his dark imagination.

He left the hotel, and started driving away. Before he reached the cutoff that led to his house, he found himself wanting to return to the hilltop overlooking Stetman's valley.

When he approached the hilltop, his hands tightened on the steering wheel. In front of him, Lea's car was parked where it had been twice before. Rage gripped him. He stopped the vehicle and, with an angry twist of his fingers, snapped the ignition off and got out. He walked toward the flat crest of the hill, his legs carrying him steadily forward while he tried to prepare for the coming confrontation.

When he finally saw Lea, he saw a stranger with her. Stopping, he gazed at her and felt the familiar sensations of rising desire. Forcefully, he shunted them aside as his anger at seeing her with someone else clouded his vision.

Walking slowly, he started toward them as they walked along the edge of the hill. As he approached them, he suddenly understood bits and pieces of their conversation.

He heard Lea speaking about the valley, and about the construction that would be done. He listened, unobserved, while she went on about how the valley would be transformed, and how the community would grow.

A different kind of rage began to consume him, an emotion so powerful that his muscles trembled under its force. Hatred glinted in his hard eyes; his lips formed a narrow, almost invisible line, and the knuckles on his hands turned a ghastly shade of white. When he was ten yards from her, she turned quickly, and he saw her eyes widen, the color drain from her face.

Darren approached them slowly, anger stiffening his stride. He stopped four feet in front of Lea, his eyes narrowed. "I'll see you in hell before I allow anyone, least of all you, to ruin this valley!"

Lea tried to shake her head in denial, but the truth of the situation was all too real. "Darren," she tried to say through bloodless lips.

"You sure did fool me, Miss Architect! But you did something far worse than fool me. You used me!"

Lea took a deep breath and drew her shoulders straighter. "I never used you, Darren, and I'm sorry you feel that way."

"Don't lie to me," he stated, his tone filled with accusation. "You used me to idle away your free time while you worked out your methods of destruction."

Lea's body stiffened further at his horrible and false charges. The love she felt for him seemed to flee under his indignant wrath. With her cheeks flaming scarlet, her breath hissed out angrily. "Don't flatter yourself!"

she snapped. "There are better ways to *idle away my free time* than by spending it with you!"

Turning quickly, she looked at Robert, whose face was devoid of expression. "I think we can continue with our work at the hotel."

Without looking at Darren, Lea headed back to the car. Robert walked by her side, as silent as he had been during the confrontation. But when they reached the car, Robert stopped and looked at her. "Who was that? And what was it all about?"

Lea wanted to pretend Robert hadn't spoken, but she couldn't. Taking a deep breath to calm her already shattered nerves, she looked back toward the hill where Darren stood. "He's a man I met when I was doing some work here," Lea began.

She paused to collect her thoughts, and then, in a low voice, continued on. "We...we dated a few times. His name is Darren Laird."

"Darren Laird, the artist?" Robert asked, his voice laced with astonishment.

"Yes," Lea answered, surprised that Robert had heard of Darren.

"He's very good. One of the best naturalist artists in the world. I own two of his works."

Lea's bitter laugh escaped before she could stop it. "I wouldn't tell him, he might steal them back from you."

Suddenly, she was aware of Robert's piercing gaze, and before she could pull her eyes from his, he spoke. "I think it was more than just a 'few dates.'"

Lea shrugged. "Whatever it was, it's over now. Besides," she said as she took her keys out of her purse, "he's the enemy. He's part of the environmental protection group that's going to try to stop the construction."

"I see," Robert said in a low voice.

Lea walked through the plaza, in the heart of Santa Fe, trying to sort out the confusion that continued to plague her. After returning from the valley, and eating a lunch she had no desire for, she and Robert had gone to the suite that she had reserved for Robert, and had started to work.

They had spent the entire afternoon going over the first of Lea's reports, transferring figures and estimates to the filing forms, and refining her previous work as they did. They'd discussed the changes in her new designs, and talked about how these accommodations to the environment would affect the project as a whole.

By eight that night, they had accomplished a fair amount, and, after eating in the hotel's dining room, Robert had told Lea that he was exhausted from the long day, as well as from the time difference between New Mexico and Washington.

After saying good night to Robert, Lea had returned to her room, but she'd known, even before attempting to undress, that sleep would not be hers for a long time. Instead of going to bed, she had left the hotel and walked the half block to the plaza, where she'd stood silently in the shadows of a building, and watched the people walking through the square.

Finally, when she could no longer stand still, Lea had stepped from her darkened vantage point, and had begun to walk by the multitude of street vendors who, surprisingly for the hour, were still doing a brisk business with the tourists.

She stopped at one spot, beneath a wooden awning, and looked at the artwork displayed in the window. Indian pottery, ablaze with bright paint, stood awaiting a purchaser. Beneath the intricate pottery, Lea saw several Indian sand paintings, and marveled at the techniques used to create them, techniques which she knew had been handed down for centuries.

Sighing, Lea started walking again, her eyes shifting everywhere, taking in everything without really seeing anything. Her thoughts were still mired in the morning's events, centered around Darren's hard insensitivity.

She felt the skin on her face tighten when she remembered the venomous stare with which he had fixed her. His hard-edged, heated, and untrue accusations had ripped through her heart with the force of a tornado, no more so because they were untrue than because of the hatred that had replaced the love she remembered having seen in his eyes.

She had never used Darren to further her goals on the project; she could never do such a thing. Yet, she almost understood how he believed she could. Almost, because if he had loved her the way he'd said, he should be able to try to understand.

Of all the men I might have met in Santa Fe, why did it have to be him? But Lea knew the answer to that. *Fate*, she whispered silently to herself, only half believing in it.

Blinking away the tears, Lea stepped off the sidewalk and crossed to the other side of the plaza. After taking only a dozen steps, she froze. The building she was standing before was an art gallery, and the single painting in its window, lit by four small spotlights, took her breath away.

The instant she saw it, she knew it for what it was—Stetman's valley. The vibrant image of the hills was filled with life. The rich colors used in the painting, and the intricate detail of the mountainsides, made it unnecessary to identify the artist by the signature—Darren Laird.

Suddenly, Lea's hands were trembling. She shook her head in denial of the emotions welling up within her, but couldn't stop their intensity. Without realizing what was happening, Lea went to the gallery door and opened it. Stepping into the cool interior, Lea smelled the burning of a light pine incense. Before she reached the center of the gallery, a young woman stepped out from the back room and favored her with a brief smile.

"May I help you?" she asked Lea.

"I...I was noticing the painting in the window. Do you have any others by the same artist?" Lea asked, holding her voice steady.

The woman shook her head, her face expressing regret. "I wish I did. No, that's the only Laird we have right now."

"I see."

"Are you interested in that painting?"

"I'm not sure," Lea replied. "How much is it?"

The woman smiled fully, taking evident joy at the question. "Nine thousand, four hundred dollars."

The amount staggered Lea. "So much," Lea whispered sadly.

"No. Actually, it's not that much. Darren Laird's paintings always go up in value. As soon as one of his paintings is bought, it grows in value by at least fifty percent of the purchase price."

Lea fixed the woman with an open stare. "I don't mean to sound doubtful, but if what you've just said is true, why are you selling it at that price, and not a higher one?"

"You're not the first person who's asked that question. The truth is that we are Mr. Laird's only gallery, and we sell his work under an exclusive agreement. Part of that agreement is that the price of each painting is fixed by Mr. Laird himself. He doesn't believe that the value of his works should be set by art critics."

"That's unusual," Lea commented. Yet she knew Darren would do something like that; it went along with his whole philosophy. "But nine thousand dollars is still not what one would call cheap."

"That's debatable, but the final price is not the one Mr. Laird sets. He gives us a price, and we add our commission—thirty-three percent."

"I see."

"Still," the woman added, "it is a bargain. As I've said, it's the last of his works available right now."

Lea gazed at the woman, and then looked toward the window. "I'd like to go outside and look at it again."

"That's not necessary. We'll be closing soon, and I have to take the painting out of the window." Saying that, the woman went to the window, lifted the painting from the easel, and brought it to the far wall where she rehung it carefully and stepped back.

Only one spotlight shone on the painting now, framing it with a gentle white glow and giving it a new life. As Lea stared at the painting, her breath caught.

"I...I'll take it," she said, her mouth dry.

"Wonderful."

"I'll have to give you a check and have the money transferred from my savings account, tomorrow."

"That will be fine. When the check clears, the painting will be yours."

"Thank you," Lea said, feeling as if she had regained just a little of what she'd lost.

"There are some forms that have to be filled out," the woman told her.

"Forms?"

"The artist's verification and a letter of agreement that states that when there is a showing of Mr. Laird's works, you will allow the painting to be a part of the showings—if Mr. Laird wants to use it—for as long as you own the painting. If you sell the painting, we must be notified so that we can make the same arrangements with the new owner."

"I see. Does that mean Mr. Laird will know that I bought the painting?"

The woman nodded. "We keep records of all purchasers of his works. Follow me, please."

Shrugging her shoulders, Lea followed the woman into her office and, after signing the forms, wrote a check for nine thousand, four hundred dollars, a sum that would leave her savings account almost bare.

After leaving the shop, Lea returned to the hotel and, when she was beneath the covers, she realized exactly what she had done. She had bought something that would add to her memories of the man she loved. Only memories would fill her lonely hours.

Sleep took a long time in coming, only to find Lea in a haunted nightmare that pitted her against Darren, in a feud that seemed to last for an eternity.

When she awoke, just as the sun was rising, Lea felt as though she had not slept at all. She lay in bed, her mind swirling with hopelessness, and tried to find the courage to surmount the shambles of her life. She fought with herself until she believed she could face the coming day and, when she felt strong enough, she left the bed and took a long, hot shower.

When she was dressed, and her hair brushed neatly into place, she called her bank in Maryland, and issued the transfer order from her savings account to her checking account, using her authorization code.

Later, after calling Robert and arranging to meet him in the dining room for breakfast, Lea left her room, determined to face the day bravely.

Darren stared at the canvas, trying to find the essence of what he had once seen in it, but failing. His mind was still captured by the dark web of deceit that he believed Lea had spun around her true identity.

Of anything she could have done to him, her sin was the worst. Shaking his head, Darren tried not to dwell on the memory of his other foolish escapade, but his defenses were weak.

She's no better than Rebecca Charlow, who at least made no pretense of what she had been after! The voice inside his head taunted him maliciously.

The depth of Lea's betrayal shook him badly, and revealed the absurdity of his love for her. No matter how hard he stared at the painting, he could not stop himself from seeing the beauty in her face, or stop from remembering how his heart and mind had opened up to her.

"Fool!" he spat to himself, shaking his head and turning from the easel. Darren forced himself to remain calm and survive Lea's lies.

Feeling his self-confidence returning, he started from the studio, his muscles telling him just how tired he was. He hadn't slept through the night; he simply hadn't been able to. He'd sat on the deck and stared at the sky, watching the stars shimmer above him. The phone had rung several times, but Darren hadn't felt like talking to anyone and had let it go unanswered. When morning had dawned he'd been no less disturbed than before.

As he reached for the door, he heard a horn outside and, opening the studio door, he saw a silver Datsun Z in the drive. A moment later, Randi and Andrew Blake emerged; in Andrew's left hand was a manila file folder, on his face was a broad smile.

Walking slowly, Darren met them halfway and gazed into Andrew's dancing eyes.

"I got it!" Andrew stated. "Don't you ever answer your phone? We've been calling all night."

"Good morning," Darren replied in a flat voice.

"You look terrible," Randi said.

"Thank you."

"Are you all right?" she asked, concern shadowing her features.

"Fine," Darren replied. Then looked at Andrew. "You got what?"

"The information about Stetman's valley. How about some coffee to go with it?" Andrew asked.

Ten minutes later, the three friends were sitting in the kitchen, sipping the coffee. "Well?" he asked.

Andrew opened the file, but didn't take out anything. "American Land Designers is a holding company, owned solely by the firm of Lansing and Mitchell, Architects. It is the company they use when they develop properties for themselves, rather than for an outside client. Lansing and Mitchell is also a highly respected firm with a good many government contracts."

"So?"

"So," Randi cut in, "when Andrew learned who they were, he, ah...broke into a few government computers and dug up some very interesting facts."

Darren stared at Randi, and then at her husband. "Broke in?"

"Not physically. You know I've always loved to play with computers. What I did was call into the different government data bases and break the code. After that, it was easy to get the information."

Darren, instead of smiling along with Andrew, shook his head. "I thought we were the good guys?"

"We are," Randi said quickly.

"Then why are we doing this illegally?"

"What other choices do we have?"

"It puts us on their level," Darren stated in a low voice.

"That's not true," Andrew argued, his tone even. "If we did everything by the rules, we wouldn't have saved a quarter of the lands that we did. If we wait until all the facts are out in the open, it'll be too late to do anything, and you damn well know that!"

Darren stared at him for a moment and tried to push his doubts aside. "I still don't like it."

"But you'll like this." Andrew withdrew a small sheaf of papers and rifled through them. "I knew there had to be some record filed of their intentions for the valley. I found it in the Federal Housing Authority's data banks."

"The FHA? They're going to put up low-cost housing in the valley?" he asked with evident disbelief.

"Not quite. They filed a prospectus for a partial senior citizens' community, looking for federal funds to subsidize part of the construction costs."

"That's normal," Darren said.

"Yes, but I dug deeper. They also filed intentions with the Department of the Interior—the Bureau of Land Management—for rights of way through the federal preserves during construction."

"We can't let that happen!" Darren declared adamantly.

"We won't," Randi assured him.

"What else did you find out?"

"I said it was a partial senior citizens' community," Andrew reminded Darren. "But I don't know what else they're planning to do with the valley. Stores, I would imagine, and a large medical and research facility to go along with the retirement population."

"That's all conjecture," Darren pointed out.

"Extrapolation, actually," Andrew said with a smile.

"That's all we have," Randi cut in. "They haven't filed anything with the state of New Mexico yet, so we're left with conjecture, or projections."

"They'll have to file soon."

The Blakes looked at Darren and waited for him to elaborate.

Darren exhaled slowly, his expression intense. "I met the architect of whatever they're building. She's a very determined woman."

"She?"

Darren's gaze grew distant, his voice likewise. "Her name is Lea Graham."

"How did you find out?"

"I met her the other day at the valley" was all that Darren was prepared to say. "What are we going to do to stop them?" he asked, changing the subject quickly.

"File suit and then bring the story to the papers."

"How can the league bring suit when it doesn't know the basis of the suit?" Darren asked.

"We've done it before. We put whatever facts we know, along with our conjectures, into the suit, and then let the builders prove we're wrong by giving a full disclosure. We did that two years ago with the Sandia Mountain Power Works, remember?"

Darren nodded slowly. "And the newspapers?"

"That's the easy part. They're always looking for controversial issues. Darren, remember, this is Santa Fe. The people here don't particularly like having a bunch of strangers moving into the area."

Darren stared at them for a moment, and then shook his head. "I don't want the valley changed. It's too important an issue, and not just because it's vacant land. Its location is strategic to the balance of wildlife in all the preserves in the area. A man-made community will interfere with the natural balance, and the animals will suffer."

Andrew held Darren's gaze as he listened to the artist's impassioned words. When Darren stopped speaking, Andrew smiled. "Of all the people in the league, you're the one who's the closest to the land. You know it in ways that most people don't." Andrew paused for a moment, his eyes suddenly out of focus. "Of course!" he half shouted to Darren. "Instead of having a reporter interview us, you should write the newspaper article. You have the power of your name to back you. Put your views in writing, Darren. Use words instead of pictures to tell the people what the results will be if this construction is allowed to take place."

Darren thought about Andrew's suggestion, and realized that his friend was right. He knew a great deal about the land, the wildlife. He had learned about the trees, and about the water that reached their interlocked root systems. He had studied the animals in the area, from mountain lions to the lowliest of rodents. He had learned their habits and the trails they followed. But only now did Darren truly understand just how much he knew.

"All right," he said to the Blakes. "I'll write an article that will make the public understand the importance of stopping the construction before it begins."

"Thank you," Andrew said.

"I want to know everything you can find out about their intentions."

"You will."

After the Blakes left, Darren sat at the kitchen table for a long time, thinking. Although he was still bothered by Andrew's tactics, he could understand Andrew's using illegal means in order to get the information.

Closing his eyes, Darren began to outline a description of the valley, stressing the importance of its ecological balance to the surrounding area. Suddenly, Lea's smiling image appeared on the backs of his eyelids.

Darren's eyes snapped open; his breath huffed angrily. "You won't beat me, Lea! You used me, and stole my love, but I'll never let you take away *my* land!"

Chapter Ten

The next two days flew by in a frenzy of last-minute
details that left Lea on the very edge of exhaustion, an
exhaustion that saved her from herself. By the time
Robert left for Washington, and they both had learned
that Jason Browning, the architectural renderer, had the
flu and had postponed his trip for two more days, Lea
was grateful for the respite.

It was early evening when she returned to the hotel
after seeing Robert off. Her first course of action was
to have her bags transferred to the suite that Robert had
insisted she take over; it had a large sitting room where
she could work.

Later after signing the check for a dinner delivered by
room service, she sat at the table and slowly ate the
sautéed trout. The memory of her first dinner with

Darren returned to haunt her, and she realized she was eating the same thing she had with him. Her fork stopped midway to her lips, and her hand trembled.

Slowly, she put the fork down and placed the silvered warming cover over the plate, her appetite gone completely. She pushed herself away from the portable table and went to the desk, where she sat down in front of the uneven piles of paperwork.

She began to separate the papers into categories. The temporary secretary she had hired for the following day would begin to type and organize the final version of the Stetman valley proposal.

An hour after she'd begun, Lea finished the chore. Sighing, she stood and ran her fingers through her hair. Going into the bedroom, Lea took her brush from the dresser and began to brush out the tangles when a knock sounded.

The instant she opened the door, a shock wave froze her to the spot. Memories of the past days flooded her senses like a surrealistic movie gone wild, turning her stomach into tensely coiling knots. Her hand tightened on the brush's handle, and her other hand rose in an effort to ward off the unexpected apparition standing in the doorway.

Staring at Darren, she slowly shook her head. "Wh-what do you want?" Lea's voice was but a dim echo of the maddening upheaval to her soul.

Darren stared at her for a long moment, taking in her unruly hair and the way her hand was held protectively before her. But he pushed away the vision of helplessness and stepped into the room before she could stop him. Once inside, he closed the door with a quick flick of his hand.

"How dare you!" Lea challenged, her temper flaring at his preemptive action. Darren didn't answer her, all he did was stare through half-lowered eyelids.

Lea, conscious of the way his chest rose and fell, sensed his anger, but that did not ease her turbulent emotions. Refusing to let him stare her down, she met his challenging and hard-eyed gaze with her own. But, when the silence dragged on, and she could no longer stand the tension, she spoke.

"Darren—"

But he cut her off quickly with his own words. "Moving up in the world, aren't you?" Darren asked, his tone as biting as his words.

Lea, puzzled at his question, could only stare blankly. "I don't understand what you mean."

Darren shook his head, his expression one of pity. "Now that the truth is out in the open, you don't have to pretend to be a vacationing tourist staying in a small room. I see that your company spares no expenses when it comes to creature comforts," he said, glancing around at the elegantly appointed room.

"What do you want?" This time, as she repeated her question, her voice held an edge of anger, and reflected none of the anguish in her heart.

"What do I want? I want to know why." he growled, stepping closer to Lea.

Unexpectedly, she shook in fear as his eyes glowered at her in accusation. Gone was the gentleness in his face that she remembered so fondly.

"Why did you lie to me?" The question was asked in a deadly tone.

In reaction to her own sudden fear of this angry, unforgiving Darren, her anger consumed her. Her lips narrowed into a tightly drawn, pale line. Her hand tightened even more on the brush, and her breathing became shallow. "I never lied to you. Never!"

"The hell you didn't!" he declared, taking another menacing step forward. When they were separated by mere inches, he spoke again. "You lied to me when you said you loved me. What you should have said was 'Thank you for letting me use you.'"

Lea felt the heat emanating from Darren's body through the thin material of her light robe. Despite the effect of his body being so close to hers, her temper overruled her desires.

"I never used you, Darren. Never!"

"You didn't?" he asked sarcastically, his words acrid to her ear. "I think that's exactly what you did. What better way to learn about the land you want to destroy? You used me, and I was stupid enough to let you."

"No, Darren! You're wrong! Or do you think I fell off those rocks just to get to meet you?" she retorted, drawing her shoulders straighter as she looked him directly in the eye.

"I think you grabbed a lucky opportunity when it was offered."

Lea said nothing, and just continued to stare. She saw a muscle throb in the side of his cheek before he spoke again.

"I took you everywhere. I showed you the beauty of the land, and shared my innermost feelings about it with you. Was it a lot of fun to hear me speak about the unspoiled land in Stetman's valley?"

"Stop it!" Lea half shouted. Tears and anger and misery welled in her eyes, but Darren would not relent.

"What was going through your pretty little head while I was telling you about the valley? Were you deciding which shops would take space in your mall? Were you going to put up little plaques in the store windows...'Shop at Maude's Boutique,' situated on the very spot of a gray fox's den?"

"You're not being reasonable!" Lea shouted.

"Reasonable? How reasonable are you?" Darren demanded in return. "For every gambel oak you cut down to make room for construction, another few trees will die because you destroyed their interlocked root system. The squirrels, birds, and other animals who live off those trees will die too. Is that what you call reasonable?"

"That's unfair," Lea said in a hushed whisper.

"So were you. I gave you honesty and truth. You gave me lies and deceit."

"I did no such thing!" Lea snapped, his last accusation inflicting more pain than she'd ever thought possible.

Darren continued to glare at her, his anger showing in the corded muscles of his neck, and in the shallow breaths controlling the rise and fall of his chest. "You betrayed my trust, and my love."

Lea stared at him, her eyes bleak under the impact of his false accusations. She shook her head again, refusing to be beaten down by his attack. But when she saw a sudden change flicker across Darren's face, a chill of warning stiffened her spine and she began to back away from him slowly.

Before she could take half a step, Darren reached for her shoulders. She tried to slip from his grasp, but Darren was too fast for her and his hands tightened cruelly on her shoulders.

"Let go of me!" she ordered. Twisting violently, Lea tried to break free of his hold.

"I thought you liked me," Darren said, his voice lowering as his eyes raked across her face. "I thought you loved me. Now you're telling me to let you go. Why?" he asked, pulling her close and crushing his mouth onto hers.

Again, Lea fought against his grasp, adrenalin giving her added strength. But her attempt to escape was to no avail against his powerful arms. Stiffening, she held her lips firm against his onslaught.

Suddenly, against her will she realized that her body was reacting to Darren, and his ruthless kiss. Hot shame burned her cheeks.

His lips were hot upon hers; his lean, strong body pressed tightly to hers was something she could not ignore. His hands burned through the thin fabric of her robe, searing the skin beneath it. Her breasts were crushed to his chest, and she could feel the racing of her blood, and the pounding of his heart.

Lea battled against the deep love she had for Darren, and against the memory of the beautiful days of sharing that had marked their short time together. *This can't be happening,* she told herself, struggling against the unwanted memories, surging emotions and desires, and the all too real feel of the man against her.

Her body and heart were betraying her in that very moment. The shame of her weakness in the face of his rage made her quick to anger. Her unconscious reaction to him ceased to exist. Fighting both Darren and herself, she held her lips immobile against the heated insistence of his cruel mouth, and her body froze even more against him. The tears spilled out, but she was oblivious to them as they cascaded down her cheeks.

Finally, Darren's grip eased. The instant she felt him relax, she spun away from his hold. Out of his reach, she turned to glare at him, his image wavering in her blurred vision.

She didn't try to control her tears, nor did she acknowledge the unmerciful pain battering her heart. All she could do was stare at him and take deep, shuddering breaths.

"Leave!" she commanded. "Get out of my room! Get out of my life!" she cried, her arms wrapping protectively about her.

"Why? Will you do the same for me? Lea, go! Take your plans and your ideas and put them somewhere else. Ruin another piece of land.... Or better yet, find something that's already been destroyed." Darren paused for a moment to take a ragged breath. His voice, when he spoke again, was low and hard-edged. "And Lea...find another man to ruin."

Stung beyond measure, Lea's neck arched stiffly and her breath hissed. Her mind ceased to function; her heart, which had been crying out its pain, shuddered at the callousness of his words.

"Is that what you think I've done to you, ruined your life?"

"You're trying your damnedest, aren't you?"

Where once electricity flowed between them, only anger and hurt could be found in its place. Lea withstood the onslaught of his stare, and of the accusations that should have never been made. But before she could find the words to make him understand how wrong he was, Darren turned his back to her and went to the door.

An instant later he stepped into the hallway and slammed the door behind him. Lea jumped at the sound; her teeth, which had been worrying her lower lip, broke the skin. The taste of blood mingled with the salt of her tears, but she was aware of neither as she stared sightlessly at the door.

Slowly, while the walls of the silent room closed in on her, Lea sank to the floor, still staring at the door, and wondered how she could have allowed herself to be so devastated by Darren—and by herself.

Lea did not sleep that night. Until sunlight flooded the streets of Santa Fe, she walked about aimlessly, trying to find some small amount of strength to help her survive the days ahead.

She knew that the love she felt for Darren would never again be returned by him. She believed that the rage and anger and cruelty were all a result of his damaged pride.

She wanted to hate him for his cold cruelty. But she realized that to hate him was impossible; she loved him.

Although he felt she had used him, Lea knew his accusations were erroneous. She tried to make herself believe that circumstance was interfering with her life, but this theory eluded her.

How could I have fallen in love with him? she asked herself over and over while the hours of the night crept slowly onward. With the sunrise, she still had no answer.

What Lea did find was a solace of sorts. The pain that had marked the night began to diminish, but not because she was getting over the incident. She was merely able to compose herself and display a good front.

After that major accomplishment, she returned to her hotel room. For the next two-and-a-half days, Lea threw herself completely into the project, working with the temporary secretary, Alicia Reynolds, to complete one final draft of the proposal.

When the secretary left for the day, Lea didn't stop working. She continually looked everything over, making minor changes in what remained to be typed. Each night she worked well past midnight until her body refused to allow her mind or eyes to function. At that point, Lea was able to fall into her bed and sleep until her wake-up call roused her.

When Jason Browning finally arrived, complete with his portable drafting table and all his other equipment, he registered at the desk. After dropping his bags off in his room, he set up his equipment in the sitting room of Lea's suite, where he planned to begin work the next day.

Late that afternoon, Lea drove Jason to Stetman's valley. Ignoring the constant reminders of Darren, she showed Jason all the future locations of the buildings.

"It's very important that your rendition of the entire valley show that most of the vegetation will remain," she said after an hour of walking and answering the artist's questions.

Then, Lea drove up to the hilly plateau overlooking the valley, and left Jason alone to work on his rough sketches.

She walked aimlessly about, alone with her thoughts for the first time since the confrontation in her hotel room. Through a chink in the barriers she had raised, Lea could once again hear his angry words, and feel the way his fingers had bitten so cruelly into her shoulders.

At the same time, she also remembered his pledge to her on this very spot, a week ago. *"We don't need any explanations, Lea. We have each other.... Whatever was in the past is no longer a part of our world."*

"Liar," she whispered to his image. "Liar," she half sobbed.

Then she sought whatever inner strength might remain. Pulling her shoulders straighter, she looked down into the valley.

You're wrong, Darren, about me and about the project, she stated silently. *And I'll damned well prove it to you.* But, deep inside she wondered if she would ever be able to prove anything to him.

She knew that he was closed-minded about any change in the environment and would fight her with every ounce of power he possessed. *What made him that way?*

Intuitively, Lea began to understand that something terrible must have happened to Darren to make him react so totally opposite to the way he had been with her originally. She sensed that the gentle and unquestioningly strong man she had fallen in love with had retreated behind an impenetrable shell. *But what caused it? Or who?*

"Lea," Jason Browning called. Lea shrugged off her tormented thoughts and turned to the artist, waiting for him to go on. "What about setting up one large bank of solar panels instead of setting them into each roof?"

Lea looked at the valley for a moment. What she saw was not the tree-studded valley floor, but the completed community that would one day be a part of the valley. "They'll stand out too much. We have to make everything look as if it was a part of the natural surroundings."

"Look at the indentation across the valley, where the two rocky slopes meet. There's no vegetation. We could set the panels on them, using raised frames so that the drainage wouldn't affect them. They'll be almost completely hidden, and they'll also pick up the reflection of the trees on the opposite slopes. It will be the next best thing to a natural camouflage."

Lea studied the inverted joining of the two slopes for several moments. But before she agreed or disagreed, she eyed the path that the cables carrying the electricity would be following, realizing that the cables could be snaked underground without damaging any of the trees.

"Okay, we'll try it out on paper and see how it looks."

Jason smiled as he nodded.

"Jason..." Lea began again, her voice low. When Jason looked at her, she took a deep breath. "It's very important to me that we take no liberties with the drawings. I want your finished work to look as much like the finished project as possible. No artistic liberties. It's important. We may have a hard fight on our hands with the ecologists."

"I've already been warned," Jason replied. "This is a pilot project to boot. You've got a lot riding on the outcome," he said in a low voice.

Lea sighed loudly. "Don't remind me."

Then she left Jason alone again to continue with his sketches of the valley. Lea was drawn once more back into her thoughts and, ignoring the pain that seemed never to abate, she tried to make herself believe that the future would ease her sorrow.

Even as she tried to convince herself of that, she felt the way Darren's hands had caressed her body, the way his lips had brought out her desire, and the way she had given her heart to him without ever thinking of the consequences.

Darren stared at the typewriter, and at his final sentence. He'd spent three days writing and rewriting until he felt that he had captured his deepest feelings.

He had written about the encroachment of civilization on the final acres of wilderness that remained in the Southwest, and described how, when people develop the land, the environment suffers.

He cited chapter and verse about the perils of endan-

gered species. His plan cried out for understanding and
for action. But he still wondered if what he had written
would help in his fight against Lea.

No! he thought adamantly, *not just against Lea, but
against anyone who tries to change the land for his own
use.*

Darren exhaled noisily and took the last sheet of paper from the typewriter. The chimes of the grandfather
clock reverberated through the house, telling him that
it was seven o'clock.

Gathering up the ten-page article, Darren put it into
a manila envelope and left the house. There was a
meeting of the executive board of the league tonight.

Less than an hour after he'd left home, Darren was
seated in the Blakes' living room. Andrew and Randi
were on the couch next to him, and Tony Velez and
Richard Dole were seated opposite.

Richard Dole, one of the founding members of the
Environmental Protection League and the president of
the Continental Federal Bank, was speaking. In his
hands was a computer printout, and as his eyes swept
across the other faces, his words rolled smoothly out.
"The firm of Lansing and Mitchell has an excellent
credit rating, and is listed highly by Dun and Brad-
street. It is a well respected architectural firm which has
worked on developments in every corner of the world."

"Too bad they didn't stay in those corners," Randi
commented.

"It is also a company that," Dole continued, ignoring Randi's sarcastic comment, "is looked upon as an
innovator of modern architectural methods and
designs."

"They sound like angels," Andrew said. "Didn't you find anything that would help us against them?"

"Perhaps," Dole responded without a smile. "Three years ago the firm was involved in a project in Oregon...." Suddenly, everyone's attention was fixed on Dole. "Lansing and Mitchell was awarded a contract by the state to construct a senior citizens' complex."

While Darren listened to Dole, his mind tried to take him back to the time before he had learned of Lea's dark secret. But he refused to be seduced by his memories, and forced himself to listen to the speaker.

"The land the state of Oregon set aside for the complex bordered a state wildlife preserve. A small ecology group, similar to ours, learned of the planned construction, and began to protest it.

"The state responded to their protests by setting up a hearing. The result was that the land was not part of the preserve, and the construction was permitted to go ahead. But," Dole said in a strong voice, "it was a situation similar to Stetman's valley in that it would disrupt the natural patterns of the wildlife.

"The land that the construction was to utilize was situated above the underground waterways that fed the preserve. Waste and pollutants from the complex would poison the water supply and, over a period of time, destroy the preserve itself.

"When evidence was presented to the state, it was ignored. The ecology group then organized protests at the construction site, disrupting the work. Because of the initial delays with the hearings, and then with the protests, construction was held up for a long enough period to make the completion of the project too expensive to continue.

"The results," Dole said in a lower voice, "were that the project was abandoned and never restarted."

"They won!" Randi declared.

Dole nodded. "And it taught the state of Oregon a lesson they won't soon forget. They lost almost half a million dollars."

"But," Darren cut in, "how does that help us against Lansing and Mitchell?"

"Everything is done on a cost basis. When a project goes too far over cost, the builders have to reevaluate their priorities. If the new projected costs are too high to make a venture profitable within a reasonable time after completion, a company will usually abandon the project and take the losses off their taxes. Lansing and Mitchell obviously do business that way."

"Are you saying that if we fail to stop the construction, then our next step will be to set up protests to disrupt their work schedule?" Darren asked.

"Exactly," Dole replied.

"Except for one thing," Darren stated, aware of the one major difference between the valley project and the one in Oregon. When everyone was staring at him, he continued. "The work in Oregon was situated over the water routes. It wasn't the construction, but the long-term use of the land, that was the danger. In Stetman's valley, it will be the construction as well as the long-term use that destroys the land. We can't even let the construction begin."

Andrew stared at Darren knowingly. "Then we'll have to do it in court! Darren," Andrew asked, "is your article finished?"

Darren nodded. "I've been thinking about our talk the other day. I don't think we should give it to the papers until we know exactly what the developers intend to do."

"It might be too late then," Dole, the banker, stated.

"Look. This company has been through protests before. Why else would they have kept their plans a secret for two years? Remember, it was only by luck that we even discovered Stetman had sold the valley. I think that if we move too soon, we may hurt ourselves."

"Their only expenses, until they start work, are the taxes on the land," Darren stated as his eyes grazed over everyone's faces. "But, if we begin our campaign against them now, all they have to do is to hold back from filing. If they put the project on ice for a year, and wait until our guard is down, then they'll be able to go ahead before we have a chance to react. No," he said emphatically, "we need to find out what they're planning. Let them file their intentions legally, and then we'll bring a class action suit to stop them completely."

When Darren ended his impassioned plea, the four other people remained silent for a few minutes. Andrew, after taking a deep breath, spoke. "I disagree; I think we should go after them now!"

Tony Velez, who had been silent until then, leaned forward. "Darren has a valid point. If the papers we file aren't completely accurate, it could hurt us."

Richard Dole studied Darren's face for a moment. "I think Darren may be right. I have to vote with Darren."

"Then it will be by vote," Randi, the organization's secretary, said. After calling for a show of hands, she looked apologetically at her husband. The vote had been four to one in Darren's favor.

Andrew accepted the verdict calmly, and his voice once again became excited. "A friend of mine works in the state clerk's office. The moment Lansing and Mitchell file their intentions, we'll know exactly what they're up to. Tony, how much of the paperwork is done?"

Tony Velez, who was the league's attorney, explained that everything was ready except for filling in the details of the construction and the exact use the builders had in mind for it.

"I hate to wait and do nothing," Andrew whispered, his tall, thin frame tense with his feelings.

Darren stared at him, but didn't see his long-time friend; rather, he was remembering Lea's note, and feeling the betrayal and deceit that had marked the end of their relationship.

Anger, directed more at himself than at Lea, firmed his resolve. "Perhaps I can force the issue," he whispered. Again, every eye was fixed on him.

"How?" Randi asked.

"By playing her game."

"Her game?" Andrew asked, puzzled.

But Darren ignored the question as his thoughts raced on. "Is the copy machine working?" he asked. The league had bought a used copier, which had proven to be as temperamental as anything that was made of flesh and blood.

"It was yesterday."

"Good. I need a copy of this article."

"What are you going to do?" Randi asked.

"Fight fire with fire. Don't ask me anything else," he stated, his expression changing into a stiff mask. "Just trust me."

A half hour later, Darren was on the Pan American Highway. The original article, along with two copies, rested on the back seat. It was almost eleven, but he had a lot more work to do before the night would end.

Throughout the silent drive, Darren's thoughts were centered on Lea. He relived the times they had spent together, and he felt the glow of passion. Even now, he still loved her. But he also remembered the disillusionment of his hopes, and knew that he could never forgive her for the treacherous blow she had dealt him with her dishonesty.

By the time he arrived home, he had worked himself into a deadly anger. Just before he sat down, he looked at his answering machine and saw the red light blinking. Flipping the switch, he waited for the tape to rewind, and then heard Carolyn Leigh's voice.

"I just wanted to let you know that we sold *View of a Valley* the other day. We're just waiting for the check to clear. The paperwork is done if you want to pick it up. Oh, don't forget, we're setting up for the new Brandewyne show that opens on Monday. I hope we'll see you then."

That was the only message. After shutting off the machine, Darren went to the typewriter and inserted a clean sheet of paper.

He felt good knowing the painting had been purchased. Although it had been the first painting of the last group of his work he'd given the gallery six months before, he had sensed it would take longer to sell than the others. He had felt that *View of a Valley* would only be bought by someone special—someone who had a feeling for the painting, beyond just wanting to own a Darren Laird landscape.

Unwilling to let the good news temper what he needed to write, Darren cleared his thoughts and thrust himself into the task at hand. Twenty minutes later he was not only finished, but satisfied with his work.

Darren stood and stretched, and then put the article, with its new addition, into a large manila envelope. When he left the house, it was to deliver the finished product to La Fonda Hotel's front desk.

"Let's see how you like being on the wrong end," he said to Lea's haunting image.

Chapter Eleven

Lea woke from yet another night of troubled dreams and sat up as she tried to push aside the heaviness shrouding her thoughts. *Will the hurt ever stop?* she wondered.

Only if I make it stop, she told herself. Strengthening her determination, Lea got out of bed to start the new day. After washing and dressing, she left the suite's bedroom. In the main room, she found that Jason was already at work; a room service cart sat in the center, a large pot of coffee and a basket of rolls on it.

"What time is it?" she asked Jason.

Jason paused, his hand poised over the drawing table as he looked at his watch. "Eight-thirty."

Lea nodded, as she poured herself a cup of coffee. Sipping it, she wandered toward Jason and glanced over his shoulder. She felt her old, confident feelings about the project. Her vision of what the valley would look like was beginning to take form on Jason's paper.

"That's looking good," Lea complimented as Jason went back to work. Rather than leave him, Lea continued to watch the artist's hand create the very vision she had been dreaming about for so long.

There was a knock on the door, and sighing, Lea went to open it to find the woman from whom she had bought Darren's painting. Lea's eyes flicked to her hands and saw she held what appeared to be the painting, wrapped in brown paper.

"I hope I didn't wake you," Carolyn Leigh said.

"Not at all, but isn't it a little early for a delivery?" she asked as she stepped back to admit the woman.

"Your check cleared yesterday afternoon, and the gallery is closing for two days while we set up for a new showing. I didn't know how long you'd be in Santa Fe, and I wanted to get the painting to you."

"That's very kind of you."

"Well, enjoy the painting," Carolyn said in parting as she handed it to her.

Lea took the large package somewhat hesitantly. When Carolyn turned back to the door to leave, Lea saw that Alicia Reynolds, her temporary secretary, had just arrived.

When Carolyn left, Alicia entered and walked directly over to Lea. "There were two things for you at the desk," she said, holding out a long, cardboard tube and a large manila envelope.

Lea put the painting down carefully and took the two objects from Alicia. The long tube contained the finished blueprints for the individual buildings. The other parcel had no markings on it except for her name.

She put the blueprints on the couch, and placed the envelope next to them. Picking up the painting, she went into the bedroom, while Alicia uncovered her typewriter and began where she'd left off the day before.

In the bedroom, Lea unwrapped the painting, her fingers trembling as she tore the paper. When the canvas was exposed, her breath caught. Slowly, she set the painting on the low dresser. Stepping back, Lea went to the other side of the room and stared at the oil rendition of Stetman's valley.

Her heart beat much too slowly, and her breathing was almost nonexistent while Darren's artistic impact overwhelmed her. She was lost within the power of the painting, and lost, too, within her memories of his love.

Her eyes misted and she was no longer seeing the gentle brushstrokes that transformed the canvas from plain material into a vibrant painting of the beautiful valley. All she saw was the image of the artist and the endless depths of his blue-gray eyes.

"You're so talented.... Why are you so unreachable?" she asked.

Once again, Lea had no answer to her question, and had expected none. All she knew was that the harder she tried to deny her feelings, the more certain she became that her love for him was not dying; her reaction to the painting was ample proof of that.

She stayed in the bedroom for several moments until she had her emotions firmly under control. When she emerged into the suite's main room, she looked at the couch again.

She picked up the cardboard tube first, and opened one end. After withdrawing the rolled blueprints, she knelt on the floor and spread them out. She studied them carefully for twenty minutes, oblivious to the sounds of the typewriter.

When she was satisfied that the draftsman had done everything accurately, she rolled the blueprints up and slipped them into the tube. Then she reached for the manila envelope. She opened the metal butterfly clasp, but as she withdrew the papers, Alicia called out to her.

Lea rose from the floor, the papers still clutched in her right hand, and went to the secretary. Standing at Alicia's side, she listened as the woman conferred with her about one section she was working on, and Lea realized that the proposal was almost completed.

Again, Lea lifted the papers. When she looked at them, she saw a brief, but neatly typed, note clipped to the front page. She read it quickly, her breath catching when she saw Darren's signature.

This is a newspaper article that will appear in the papers the day after you file the intention to build in Stetman's valley.

Darren.

Pulling the note free, she read the words typed at the top of the first page. Her pulse started to beat erratically, and her mind turned cold.

Without a word, she walked out of the room and into her bedroom, closing the door behind her. Sitting on the edge of the bed, Lea continued to stare at the title of the paper, a sinking sensation building in the pit of her stomach.

THE RAPE OF OUR HERITAGE
By Darren Laird.

Lea forced herself to read the typed pages. While her eyes took in every word, part of her worked furiously in rebellion at what she was reading.

Remarkably, she absorbed everything that Darren, in his all too biased way, had written. Like the artist he was, he used his words the way he used his brushes, to paint a startling picture that made it seem as if the valley were indeed about to be ravished.

He used impassioned pleas to capture the reader's thoughts, and Lea could almost feel her own objections rising at his description of what was going to happen to the valley. The truth of what she was doing, and had been doing, helped her to defend herself against Darren's prejudiced, false views.

When she finished the final pages, her mind spun dizzily. She had to close her eyes in order to stop herself from crying out. She held her eyes shut for several moments until she managed to instill a semblance of control over herself.

The words she had just read blazed dangerously in her mind. They were inflammatory and, for the most part, false. Darren was using his name and his vision of what the world should be to fight her. Worse, he was doing it without any real knowledge of the plans for the valley.

Lea tried to use logic in an effort to discover the reason for Darren's unyielding stand. She replayed the things he had said to her, and the charges he had raised against the project. With a swiftness that took her by surprise, Lea suddenly realized the truth.

She saw now that it was not just the valley that Darren was fighting; he was also striking out at her personally, attacking her because of what had happened between them. His blatant and harassing charges against her held no truth or merit at all. Yet to those who would read the newspaper article, she would seem to be a cold, calculating woman bent on changing the environment and bringing competition to the business people in the area as well as hurting the grandeur of Santa Fe's surrounding lands, turning them into urban eyesores.

Lea knew she had no recourse against this article. To fight him openly, especially at the same time that they filed their intentions for the valley, would only bring on more problems with the public in general.

Shaking her head, Lea turned on the bed and reached for the telephone. Her hand hovered above it for a time, while she tried to think of a way out of this new and potentially disastrous situation.

Slowly, she pulled her hand back. She couldn't call Robert and tell him about the article—not yet. The best the company could do at this stage would be to have a lawyer file an injunction against the newspaper before the article was printed.

If they took that action, the newspaper could easily print the article while their own lawyer used legal maneuvers to delay the injunction. Once the article was printed, the damage would be irrevocable, and the retraction the paper would be forced to print would never undo the harm.

No, I have to find a way to stop it! But how?

Then Lea looked at the article again, and she felt herself growing angrier at the one-sided words, and at the unfair methods he used to manipulate the reader's emotions. Her rage grew out of bounds at the prejudiced, unfeeling assault against her personally. Between the lines of what he had written, Lea felt other factors at play. His attack against her was a rejection to the love he had claimed to have for her. It was also his way of hurting and punishing her for something she'd had no control over.

As the knowledge of what Darren was trying to do continued to fill her senses, her own determination swelled. She promised herself that she would prove to Darren that he was wrong, and that his charges against her were false.

Placing the typewritten pages face down, Lea tried to think of a method to fight him. An hour later she had worked out her idea, and she had become increasingly confident that her idea might be the only hope that her project had. Lea also realized, after rereading Darren's damning article, that in order to stop it, she would have to change his mind completely about the project, and about her.

Standing, Lea finally left the confines of the bedroom and returned to the main room. She stood in the center of the room for a few silent minutes. Then she went over to the secretary, who was still working at her fast pace.

"How long until it's done?" she asked Alicia.

Alicia didn't take her eyes from the pages on the paper stand, nor did her fingers slow on the keys. "Another hour at the most."

"Good," Lea said with a nod that the woman did not see. "When you're done, I'll need three copies, and two of them have to be bound."

"When?" Alicia asked, still not looking up from the typewriter.

"Today," Lea stated.

This time Alicia paused to look at Lea, and smiled apologetically. "This is Santa Fe, not a big city. I don't know if I can get it done today."

"What about Albuquerque?" Lea asked quickly.

"Possibly, but it's Friday. The copy and printing places that are big enough to handle this job may not be able to do it today. I did tell you that we would have to arrange for the work in advance, so there would be no problems," Alicia reminded her.

"When you're finished, see if you can find a place, okay?"

"I'll try," Alicia promised, but she didn't sound hopeful.

Lea shrugged and went back to the room service cart and poured herself a fresh cup of coffee. When she had hired Alicia, she'd explained about the delicacy of the work, and that when it was done, the proposal had to be copied and professionally bound, but couldn't be left overnight at the copier's. Alicia hadn't thought that it would be a problem then. But Lea also understood what Alicia had just told her. It was Friday, and it would be afternoon before the proposal was ready for copying.

I'll find a way, she told herself confidently.

Darren picked up the telephone and dialed the gallery's number. On the fourth ring, Carolyn Leigh answered.

"Hello, Carolyn, it's Darren."

"How are you?" she asked.

"Alive.... Listen, is *View of a Valley* still at the gallery?"

"No, I delivered it this morning, just before we started to set up for the new show. Why, is there a problem?"

"Not really. I wanted to take a picture of it to use for a newspaper article."

"Are you being interviewed again?" Carolyn asked.

"No, this is for an article I'm writing."

"I don't think the buyer has left Santa Fe yet. If you want, I can call and ask to photograph the painting," Carolyn offered.

Darren paused for a moment. This morning he'd thought of putting a photograph of the valley in with the article. At the same time, he'd felt that no photograph, reproduced on newsprint, could possibly portray the beauty. Instead, he'd realized that his painting might reproduce better, if the buyer was still in Santa Fe.

"What's the name? I'll give him a call."

"Her, Darren. Why do you always think that it's only men who buy your paintings?"

"Only a figure of speech," he said honestly, smiling at Carolyn's reaction.

"Lea Graham," she said.

The smile froze on Darren's lips. His hand tightened on the receiver, and a red film of anger blinded him.

"Darren?" Carolyn asked when he remained silent.

"Why her?" he asked in a low voice.

"I don't understand," Carolyn said.

Darren shook the fog from his thoughts and took a deep breath. "Nothing, I didn't say anything. Thank you, Carolyn, good-bye."

After he hung up, he turned and stared out at nothing. Once again, she'd betrayed him, trespassed on his life.

Suddenly, he couldn't sit still, and left the house. He got in his Land Rover and drove away, trying to ease the anger and frustration.

At two in the afternoon, Lea returned to the hotel, annoyed at herself for having wasted time in a futile search. Her attaché case was weighted down by the proposal, but only that, since she had been unable to get a copy made.

After deciding on her course of action, she had called Robert Kanter and told him that she feared the ecology group might try to disrupt their work sooner than anticipated. She'd also told him the proposal had been finished, and all they had to do was get it copied.

Robert had been concerned about the ecology group, and was delighted to hear of Lea's progress. They'd talked for a little while longer, and Robert had agreed with Lea that they should file the proposal, the first thing on Monday morning, if possible.

After Lea's phone call to Robert, Alicia had spent an hour on the telephone, calling various copying and printing businesses in Albuquerque, only to be told that they were too busy to accommodate a rush job of two hundred pages; it would have to wait until Monday.

One copy business told Alicia that, although they couldn't do the work that afternoon, they could make copies the next day and have them bound and ready by Saturday afternoon. Lea had told Alicia to make the arrangements, but she still refused to give in about getting at least one copy today—that was as important as anything else she had to do.

Giving Alicia several typing chores, Lea had gone out in the hopes of finding a place where she could have the proposal copied. The three businesses she located had all apologized for being unable to do a rush copy, but had promised her that if she left the work with them, they would have it ready by Monday evening.

With the knowledge that she would have the bound copies by Saturday afternoon, Lea had thanked the men and left: Monday would be too late. Lea believed that she would have to force the issue by filing the intentions Monday morning, whether or not Darren Laird eased his position.

Sighing, Lea stepped into the lobby of the hotel. As she walked past the reception desk, she almost stumbled. The office door was open, and a young woman was standing at a small, old-fashioned copying machine, waiting for it to duplicate whatever she had put into it.

Lea turned to the desk clerk and walked over to him. When she stood before him, he looked up. "Can I help you, Miss Graham?"

Smiling, Lea nodded. "I hope so." Then she explained that she was in a difficult bind, and that she had to have some work copied immediately. "Would it be possible to use your machine?"

The clerk looked uncomfortable for a moment as he met her pleading eyes. "Well, it's not something we usually encourage...."

"It really is important, and of course I'll pay for the material I use."

"It's an old machine," he said.

"I don't care if it was built before electricity was discovered! As long as it works, I need it."

The clerk finally smiled at her. "It's not quite that old." Relenting, he led Lea into the office just as the woman using the machine left. The clerk showed her how to operate the almost obsolete machine, and when she withdrew the thick sheaf of paper from her attaché case, the clerk's eyes almost disappeared behind his lids.

"I promise I'll be gentle with the machine," Lea said with a soft, if somewhat victorious, smile.

After he saw that she was doing everything correctly, the clerk returned to the front desk, and left Lea to her labors.

Because of the type of copier it was, each copy had to be covered with a sheet of special paper that an image was copied onto. After that, the copied paper was put through another part of the machine, and only then was a reproduction of the original printed. It was a long, tedious, and mindless job that took her almost three hours to complete. But when it was over, Lea felt a sense of accomplishment.

The first step in her plan was done. After returning to her room, Lea arranged for Alicia to pick up the proposal in the morning and bring it to the copier, where she would wait with it until it was finished.

Then, with Alicia gone for the day, Lea went over to Jason and looked over what he'd already done.

"It's perfect," she whispered. "You're really doing a wonderful job."

"Thank you," Jason said, not looking up from his work.

"Can you have it done for Monday morning?"

Jason froze. He straightened on the stool and turned to look at her. "Monday?"

"We have to file Monday morning."

Jason shrugged. "I'll try."

"That's all I can ask," she replied.

When Jason returned to his work, Lea went into the bedroom and spread out the copy of the proposal. Working slowly, she compared everything Darren had written, and, wherever it was appropriate, highlighted the corresponding sections of the proposal with a yellow marker.

Then she neatly stacked the sheets of paper and sighed loudly. "All right, Darren Laird, I'm ready for you now!" she declared. *I hope,* she added in silent prayer.

When she emerged from the bedroom, she saw that Jason was still hard at work. Walking toward him, she felt sharp pangs of guilt because she knew she was responsible for his being at the drawing table for eleven straight hours. "Are you going to call it a day?" she asked when she was closer to him.

Jason looked at her over his shoulder. "I think I have to, everything's getting blurry," he admitted, stretching his arms above his head to ease his straining muscles.

Looking closely at him, Lea saw that his eyes were red with fatigue. "Why don't you take a shower and meet me in the dining room for dinner?"

"You got a deal," Jason replied. Five minutes later, his equipment was put away and he started toward the door.

"Jason," Lea called, stopping him just as his hand reached the knob.

Turning, Jason looked at her and waited.

"I just want to thank you for working so hard on this project. It means a lot to me."

Jason brought his hands together in front of him, and took a deep breath. "Lea, this project means a lot to me, too, and to all of us—the younger people at the company, the ones who started at the same time as you did.

"Ever since you pulled that little trick to get yourself put in charge of the project, we've been behind you. What you're trying to do here is important to us, because some of us, like you, believe that we can create communities that will enrich the areas they're in instead of destroying them. The old ways of building are beginning to fade, and we want what you—and we—are doing to be the new wave of the future."

Lea stared at him, trying to understand what had motivated Jason to speak the way he had. Although she'd known him since she'd started working at Lansing and Mitchell, and had worked frequently with Jason, she had never expected this reaction.

"I didn't realize that anyone else was interested in what I was doing," she admitted.

"Maybe it's time to open your eyes and take notice of what's happening around you." Although Jason's voice was light, his words struck a deep chord in her.

Slowly, as she continued to gaze at him, she nodded. "Perhaps it is," she whispered, thinking about her tendency to fix her energies on the job she had to do, and not look around at what else was happening in the world. "Jason...thank you."

"I'll see you in the dining room in a little while," he said.

A moment later he was gone, and Lea put the highlighted copy of the proposal in her attaché case, closed it, and then returned to the bedroom where she changed for dinner, still pleased with Jason's compliments.

As she dressed, she suddenly felt a sense of responsibility to Jason, and to everyone else who was standing behind her in her efforts to make this project not only a success, but an important step forward in architectural design.

After having a pleasant and informative dinner with Jason, whom she had asked to explain more fully exactly which people at the company he had spoken of earlier, Lea returned to her room and started to prepare for what she must do that night. Her confidence was buoyed by Jason's belief in her.

As she thought about her idea and plan to make Darren change his mind about the project, she suddenly paused in her thoughts. *If he changes his mind about the project, will he change it about me?*

That thought sent a cold chill racing along her spine. She remembered their two past confrontations, both of which had shown her Darren's unrestrained rage. But it was the last time they had met, when he'd barged into the suite, his hatred for her ablaze on his face and laced within his words, that gave her the answer to her question.

No, she told herself, *whatever hurt him in the past will not let him forgive me for what I didn't tell him.*

Shaking her head at the sadness of her thoughts, Lea steeled herself to do what was necessary. Walking into the main room, she picked up her attaché case and left the suite.

The drive went all too quickly, and once she reached Darren's cutoff, Lea drove slowly up the dark mountain road, her headlights flooding the road and pointing the way. The closer she got to his house, the more nervous she became.

She wondered if he would even open the door when she knocked. She was afraid he wouldn't listen to anything she had to say. She remembered that last glaring stare he had fixed her with before he'd walked out of her room. She felt his anger, and made herself feel her love for him in an effort to strengthen her resolve.

Finally, when his drive was illuminated in the headlights, Lea sighed and stopped the car. She knew all she had to do was turn the steering wheel and press down on the accelerator. But something was stopping her. She thought about the years she had invested, not only in this project, but in achieving the dreams and goals she had believed herself destined to reach.

Her hands tightened on the steering wheel, and her foot pressed gently on the gas pedal. The car started forward; Lea began to breathe again.

It was either two minutes, or three lifetimes later—Lea was never able to remember how long it actually took—when she stopped the car next to Darren's Land Rover and shut off the engine.

She stared at the house, and at the single light glowing through the living room window. Purposefully, she opened her attaché case and withdrew the copy of the proposal. Then she left the car.

When she reached the door she took a deep, preparatory breath, raised her left hand, and knocked. After waiting a full minute under the barrage of her screaming nerves, Lea knocked again. When there was still no answer she stepped back, sighing half with regret, half with relief.

At the bottom of the stone steps, she paused to look at Darren's studio. Lights blazed powerfully from the windows, and Lea's stomach tightened nervously.

Aware of the magnitude and importance of what the project meant to her, and to the other people working on it, Lea started toward the studio. When she reached the door, she raised her hand to knock, but stopped when she saw the door was partially open.

With her lower lip caught between her teeth, Lea pushed the door fully open and stared into the studio. She saw Darren, standing sideways to her, at his easel, his head cocked to one side as he studied his work, oblivious to anything else.

Slowly, silently, Lea started inside. But after only two steps, she stopped.

"Darren," she called, her voice almost breaking under the stress of speaking his name.

She saw Darren's shoulders stiffen, and when he whirled to face her, Lea almost gasped at his tight features and clouded, unyielding eyes.

"We have to talk," she said a moment later.

Chapter Twelve

Standing boldly against the menacing glare Darren directed at her, and battling the tide of her emotions at seeing him again, Lea forced herself to breathe calmly and walk toward him.

Before she was halfway to him, Darren started away from the easel. "What are you doing here?" he asked in a strained voice.

"Didn't you expect the cold and unfeeling woman who is the heartless and dark harbinger of destruction to come here after you left the article at the hotel for me to read?" she asked, fighting hard to maintain her level tones and not let bitterness seep into her words. When she was a half dozen feet from him, she stopped. "Or was that another Lea Graham you were describing in your article?''

"I expected you to see the truth of what you're planning to do, and to understand that I'll never permit it to happen." Darren continued to challenge her with his hostile glare for several seconds.

"The truth of what I'm planning?" The question shot from Lea's lips like an arrow. Until that very moment, she hadn't known what she would say to him. All she did know was that she was being attacked on every level by his very presence, and that if she faltered, all would be lost. "You don't know what the truth is. You're so blinded by your prejudices that you won't let yourself differentiate between truth and your own opinions."

"Why did you buy my painting?" he asked suddenly, ignoring her accusation.

Lea stared at him for a long moment, her pulse racing. "Because it's a beautiful painting, filled with life. It's also a memory for me of a kind and understanding man whom I fell in love with. A man whose talents surmount his failings."

"I want the painting back," Darren stated.

Lea stiffened. "No." The single word was spoken softly, yet the steel will behind it told Darren of its finality.

"Get out!" Darren ordered, his eyes again narrowing into dark, glaring orbs.

"When I'm ready!" Lea retorted, her own anger lending her the strength she needed to fight him and fight *for* him.

"Do you think that you can just walk into some-one's life and take control of it?" Darren asked. Al-though his face remained fixed in a half scowl, the pain that was again emerging was growing stronger.

"I never did that to you, Darren," Lea whispered, slowly shaking her head in emphasis.

"Didn't you? Perhaps I used the wrong words," he said in a husky, sarcastic tone. "You used me, Lea. And when you got all the information you needed, you dis-carded me."

Lea's eyes widened under his painful and false accu-sation. Her rage built quickly, but it was tempered by the truth that enabled her to hold it at bay. "You ego-tistical...I tried to tell you about myself. More than once!"

"When?" he half growled, half shouted.

Lea's eyes swept across his face. Her emotions rolled wildly while she drank in his handsome features. Her voice, when she finally spoke, was heavy with regret. "The first time you made love to me, I wanted to tell you that I wasn't on vacation, that I wasn't who you thought I was."

"Why didn't you? Were you too taken with pas-sion?" he demanded acidly.

"You bas—" she began, hurt badly by his disdain-ful and cutting remark. But Lea held back her retort, knowing that anger would only cause more anger. Lea took a long, shuddering breath. "You wouldn't let me. I tried, but you stopped me."

Darren shook his head stubbornly and his voice was husky. "Perhaps you did try to tell me, in your own mind at least, but you never said anything. No, Lea, you used me, and made a fool out of me. But you won't do that to me anymore."

"I really believed you loved me," Lea whispered as tears threatened to spill from her eyes. Forcefully, she willed them away as she gazed at him.

"Do you think I tell every woman I meet that I love her?" Darren's question was accented by a flash of pain she saw cross his eyes.

"I wouldn't know about that," Lea stated.

Darren's strained breathing was loud in the air. The muscles in his shoulders knotted, and a vein throbbed mightily in the side of this neck. "I believe you," he said at last. "But, I don't think you know very much at all about real emotions—just your job!"

Lea's cheeks flamed scarlet. Her mind spun in an angry and dizzying battle that pitted her heart against her logic. An eternity later, Lea exploded at Darren. "And all you know about is your painting! You shout about the beauty of nature so that everyone can hear. But that isn't really what you're saying. No, Darren, what you're saying is 'Look at me. See how perfect I am because I can show you something beautiful. Love me!'"

"I suppose you're a psychologist too?" he asked sarcastically.

Lea blinked. "No," she whispered, "I'm just the person who loves you...despite yourself."

"I doubt that," Darren snapped.

Unexpectedly, Lea detected a haunting undertone to his words, an undertone that had been present since she'd stepped into the studio. She stared at him with newfound insight, her heart beating much too fast. "No, Darren, I don't think you do doubt that I love you. I think you doubt yourself. I think it's you who's afraid of your emotions and that makes you hide behind your art."

"I wasn't hiding when I made love to you. You knew who I was! But you were hiding beneath an unspoken lie!"

"I was not!" she yelled, denying his unjust accusation.

"Yes, dammit, you were hiding behind a mask of dishonesty. You made me believe that you loved me, while you sneaked behind my back and attacked the things that are most important to me."

"Perhaps they are just as important to me," Lea whispered, closing her eyes for a moment against the hatred naked on Darren's face. When she opened them again and gazed at him, she knew that she had to try one more time to make him understand.

"You can think what you want to about me," she told him in a low, determined voice, "but at least admit one thing."

"What?" he snarled.

"That it's not the valley project, but me, who you're fighting against."

"They're one and the same thing!"

"Are they? Your article was eloquent, Darren, but it was all conjecture. You have no idea of what we're planning to build there, or how we'll build it. But those last three pages told me all I have to know. It's me you're trying to destroy!"

"That's ridiculous," Darren countered, refusing to accept or yield to her statement.

"Is it? Something... No, I think some*one* hurt you very badly once, and now you think I'm trying to do the same."

"Are you an architect or a shrink?" Once again, his question was laced with sarcasm.

Lea sighed gently. "I'm a woman, Darren, that's all."

"No," he said quickly, "that's not all."

Sadly, Lea realized that the overwhelming love she felt for him would never be enough to make him understand her. "I feel sorry for you," Lea whispered at last.

"You feel sorry for me?" Darren asked, astonished at her choice of words. "For what? For believing you were someone I could love?"

Lea's eyes turned into burning orbs as she withstood his emotional verbal attack. Then her own rage burst outward, and she retaliated.

"Don't talk to me about love! You don't know the meaning of the word. Love is understanding and forgiveness and acceptance of another. It is not the imposing of a personal ideology as a prerequisite for that acceptance."

Darren stiffened again at the words that seemed to drive directly into his heart. "Are you finished?" he asked coldly.

"Am I?" Lea asked, refusing to accept the defeat she had just realized was all that was left for her. "Darren, when we watched the eagle, I wanted to tell you about myself and what I was doing here."

"Why didn't you?"

"Before I could, you told me that you had learned about the valley, and what was going to be done there. Your unreasoning anger stopped me. But even then I tried.... Do you remember when I said that other people are entitled to share the beauty?"

Darren thought back to that afternoon, and to the hypothetical argument they'd had. *Not so hypothetical...*he repeated silently to himself. He nodded in answer to her question.

"You wouldn't listen to anything I had to say. Whenever I raised a point, you shrugged it off. You aren't interested in what can be done with the valley, good or bad, only in what you think should not be done."

"You have no idea of what I'm interested in," he told her in a temper-ridden voice.

"Don't I? I'll tell you what you're interested in. You're interested in your art to the exclusion of anything and anyone else. Your sight is nothing more than tunnel vision, directed only at what you see, and how you see it. Other people don't count."

"Really?" he asked, his anger intensifying. "Suppose you tell me what you see."

Suddenly Lea smiled. It was a tight smile, not of victory, but of finally getting a chance. "All right, Darren, I'll do just that!"

Before continuing, Lea held up the copy of the proposal. Then she turned and went to a small counter at the side of the studio. She put the papers on it and turned back to face Darren.

"That is a copy of what I...we intend to do with the valley. It's for you to read, and to think about when I'm finished telling you what I came here to say."

Lea paused, waiting to see some reaction on Darren's face, but all she saw was the unbreachable stoicism immobilizing his features.

"As I already told you, I'm an architect. But I'm also a community designer. The two are not necessarily the same; they are more comparable to the way a sculptor and a painter are both artists, but work in different media.

"As the architectural designer of the valley project, I'm in charge of developing a community here, but it's a different type of community than has ever been attempted on this scale.

"You could almost call it an experiment in living. I'm trying to... No, dammit, I am going to create an intergenerational community where young families live side by side with retired couples. Both need a place to live that's peaceful. The older people have a right to enjoy their remaining years, surrounded by beauty, rather than being encased in rigid retirement communities that make them want to give up on the future and think only about their 'good years'—the past.

"The younger families, the ones just starting out in life, should also have a chance to learn how to live outside the firm structures of the cities and suburbia, where they and their children can learn to appreciate, and not to abuse, the land that's around them."

Giving voice to her dreams, Lea continued on, ignoring the unemotional mask that was Darren's face. "The older residents, although retired, will have a reason for living and enjoying each and every day—that is, the children. What we're hoping for is that the retired people will be surrogate grandparents to the children, working with them after school or taking care of the preschoolers in a day-care environment. The older residents will gain from the children, just as the children will gain from them. Because the children will be exposed to the experience of the retired people, a large burden will be lifted from the parents, a burden that urban living puts on them in the first place.

"Darren, I want to give people a chance to live with nature, not to take control of nature and reshape it to suit someone's ideal of how people should live their lives. My plans call for the construction to utilize the valley's natural setting, and not deface it," she informed him as her voice faded and silence once again reigned in the studio.

With Lea's impassioned description at an end, Darren continued to stare at her. Her words struck certain chords in his mind, even as he tried to deny them. "It all sounds very pretty, just like the way you sounded to me, before I really knew you."

"Before you really knew me?" Lea challenged, her anger surfacing at his latest affront. "That's really too bad, because you never knew me! Or, is it that you're so...so macho that you can't accept anyone else's visions? Only yours is a perfect vision; only something that the great Darren Laird can see, can create, is good!"

"I won't be seduced by you, or by your plans," Darren retorted, his voice low and threatening. "Please leave, Lea."

"Read the proposal, Darren," she said.

"It won't make any difference," he replied.

"Probably not," Lea agreed. "After all, how could I expect you to look at it with an open mind after the way you put your prejudices on paper in an effort to destroy something good that is trying to be accomplished, as well as libelling me personally with such single-minded vengeance?"

"I'm doing what I have to," Darren stated in a flat voice.

Closing her eyes for a moment, Lea nodded. "Of course you are," she whispered. When the words faded, Lea opened her eyes, turned from him, and went to the door. Before she opened it, she glanced back over her shoulder. "I'm sorry, Darren."

"Don't be!" he snapped. Then he turned away from her, and started back toward his easel.

Watching him walk away, Lea refused to accept what was happening. "But I am sorry, Darren, for falling in love with somebody who can't, or won't, accept my love for what it is!" Without waiting for a reply, Lea opened the door and stepped into the night.

Outside, she took several deep breaths of the cool mountain air, forcing back the tears that threatened to escape. A heavy cloud of sadness settled around her, and her thoughts whirled randomly in her mind.

Lea knew that she had done her best, but was afraid that her best wasn't good enough. Stopping, she turned back to look at the studio.

"Whatever it takes, I'll find it. I'll fight you, Darren, I won't give up!"

On what? she asked herself suddenly. *Am I talking about the project, or Darren?* Lea realized she wasn't quite sure of the answer to that question.

Darren refused to turn and reply to her final remarks. Instead he walked to the easel and stood there until he heard the studio door close. Only then did his eyes travel back to the spot from where she had disappeared.

After an unknown amount of time, Darren glanced at the canvas he'd been working on. His breathing was steady, and didn't reflect the emotional turmoil her visit had stirred within him.

Then he looked at the counter where she'd put the proposal. *My plan worked,* he told himself, but he felt no sense of elation or victory.

Again, Darren studied the painting that Lea hadn't seen. He felt all the powerful feelings she had evoked within him rise up while he studied the contours of her face as he had painted them.

Her perfect reflection, superimposed upon the valley, stirred his heart without his wanting it to. Although every line of the valley could be seen beneath Lea's image, it was her face that dominated the canvas.

Above her image, in the upper left corner, lightly outlined but not yet painted, was the golden eagle they had watched for hours. He had sketched it, showing its full wingspan as it soared high above the valley, and above Lea.

On the rocks where Lea had sat, the collared lizard no longer appeared menacingly startled; rather, it was staring up at Lea's face. Darren had painted Lea's large, almond-shaped eyes as if they were gazing toward the eagle. Specks of gold and green gave them life.

Closing his mind to his inner feelings, Darren lifted a brush and dipped it into the palette. Carefully, he began to paint the eagle's wings, accenting their might as he detailed the magnificent feathers.

While he worked, his emotions rose up to battle with him and hold him back from completing the painting. When Lea's features, stiff and pain-filled as they had been moments before she'd left, floated in the air between the canvas and his eyes, he thought about what she'd said tonight. Darren's breath heaved angrily out. He drew his arm back, and then whipped it forward.

"Damn it all!" he shouted as the brush cartwheeled in the air, flying madly toward the far wall. When it hit the wall, bristles first, a blob of paint marked the spot it struck.

Moving stiffly, Darren went over to the counter and picked up the proposal Lea had left. Then he shut off the lights in the studio and went to the house.

Sitting at the kitchen table, he started to read. He gave his full attention to the proposal, and did not skip a single word of Lea's plan.

After reading the first fifty pages, the words began to swim on the pages. Standing, he left the table and made himself some coffee. He drank the first cup outside on the deck, and then poured a second, and returned to the proposal.

But again the words were moving over the pages, and he was unable to catch a single one and understand its meaning. Darren shook his head and gathered the papers together. He stood, left the table, and went into the front hallway. There, he took out a heavy flannel shirt, left the house, and went to the Land Rover.

He drove slowly toward Stetman's valley. He did not stop at the entrance; instead, he drove carefully over the valley floor, his headlights illuminating the trees and turning them into ghostly creatures.

When he reached the center of the valley floor, he stopped the Land Rover, shut off the headlights and ignition, and leaned back in the seat. The night was alive with songs. The insects and night birds filled his ears with their music. He stayed like that for several minutes, until he finally left the vehicle, and walked nearby.

The fragrance of the valley, and the sounds within it, filled his senses. He thought of the way it looked in daytime, and the way it appeared at night. Darren knew that he loved this land in a way that few could understand, but it was enough for him to be able to understand it himself.

After walking aimlessly about for almost an hour, Darren returned to the Land Rover and sat in the back seat. He leaned his head back, and closed his eyes.

The instant he did, Lea's face reappeared in his mind. Her beautiful features were boldly accented; her soft eyes were like two deep whirlpools of ever-changing color. Loss filled him suddenly, making him aware of just how much he loved her, and of how hard it had been to hold back his emotions when she had been near.

Her words, defending both herself and the project, echoed in his mind, and while he heard them again, he tried not to listen to what she was saying.

"I can't," he whispered. But his denial did not stop the memory. "Someone hurt you badly, and now you think I'm trying to do the same" was her taunting reasoning.

"Not trying, you're doing..." Darren whispered to her image. But his words did help him, and as he continued to fight against his feelings, sleep stole unexpectedly over him. While he slept, serenaded by the soothing music of animal life in the valley, no dreams of Lea came to disturb his rest.

When Lea awoke from yet another restless night of troubled sleep, she went into the suite's main room, where she found Jason already at work. Not ten minutes later, Alicia Reynolds came to pick up the proposal.

After instructing Alicia to bring the bound copies to Randolph Hastings, the New Mexican architect whose seal would be affixed to the proposals in accordance with the local and state laws, she reminded the secretary never to let the documents out of her sight.

When Alicia left, Lea ordered coffee for herself and Jason, and breakfast for him. Her appetite seemed to have permanently vanished. Then she went over to Jason and silently watched as he worked, amazement settling in her mind at the accuracy with which he had transformed her designs to an almost finished picture.

When breakfast came, and Lea and Jason were sitting across from each other, Jason studied her intently. "You look terrible," he commented.

"Thank you," Lea replied sarcastically.

"What's wrong?" he asked suddenly.

Lea shook her head slowly, but said nothing.

"Before this, we were acquaintances—friendly co-workers if you will. But after the last few days, I'd like to think that we've become friends."

Lea stared at him for a moment, gazing into his warm brown eyes. Then she smiled as she realized the truth of what he'd just said. "We have become friends," she replied.

"And friends are there to help. Trust me, Lea. What's bothering you?"

Without consciously deciding to speak to Jason, she found herself uncharacteristically opening up to him. She explained the situation they faced, and told him what she had done to try and salvage their work. Yet, while she told her story, she did not once speak of love, or of the deep personal relationship that had formed between her and Darren; rather, she spoke of him as a recent acquaintance with whom she had formed a friendship. She spoke for a long time, and when she had nothing else to say, she finished with a simple "And that's it."

Jason's face was set in tense lines, his brown eyes reflecting compassion. "Maybe he'll see what we're trying to accomplish when he reads the proposal."

"I don't think he will. He's too closed-minded—too set in what he thinks we're trying to do," Lea told him.

Jason continued to study her for several more seconds. "Lea, what happened between you and Darren Laird? And I don't mean about the project." With that question, Lea, although she had tried her best to keep her voice unemotional throughout her story, knew she had failed, and that Jason had seen through her front.

"I made a mistake," she admitted. When Jason said nothing, she went on. "I fell in love with him." Once again, Lea found herself unburdening her emotions on Jason. When there was nothing left to say, she gazed silently at her friend and waited for him to speak.

"From everything you've told me, it sounds like he fell in love with you, too."

"So he says... But I don't believe him. And," she added in a stronger voice, "it doesn't matter anymore whether he did or not."

Jason smiled. "Of course it doesn't. That's why you've had those dark shadows under your eyes ever since I arrived here. Be honest with yourself, Lea, you're the only one who can be."

Lea smiled hesitantly at Jason. She reached across the table and grasped his hand in both of hers. "Thank you, Jason, for listening to me."

"As I said before, that's what friends are for. Besides, I wouldn't give up hope just yet. We've still got until Monday morning for Laird to change his mind."

Lea nodded without any real conviction as Jason stood and stretched.

"I better get back to work. I'll have the overall view finished in an hour or so."

"Wonderful," Lea said, an animated smile crossing her face for the first time in days.

"And if we're lucky, I'll have the last piece done by tomorrow afternoon." With that, Jason returned to his artist's table.

Lea stayed in her chair, her mind searching for something to do. But she realized that after two years of nonstop work, she was almost finished with the first phase and, except for filing the intention to build on Monday, would have to wait until construction began before she could do anything else on the project.

This knowledge did her absolutely no good, and refusing to accept the fact that she had nothing to do, she remembered the photographs she'd brought in to have developed.

Standing, Lea told Jason she would be back in a little while. When she left the hotel, she went to the plaza, and to the small photography store situated in a large, multi-use building that comprised several restaurants and shops.

When she emerged into the daylight again, she held three envelopes of developed film securely in her hand. As she walked back to the hotel, she opened the first set of pictures and gazed at the various views of Stetman's valley.

Although she'd already taken more than enough pictures of the valley on her previous trips, those photos had been for work; the pictures she was looking at now had been taken for her own pleasure.

By the time she reached the hotel, she had gone through the first two sets of photographs. But when she opened the third set, her step faltered, and she leaned against the side of an adobe-faced building.

As she stared at the first photo, her breath caught, and a misty veil floated between her eyes and the picture of Darren's handsome face. She took several calming breaths, but did not leave the security of the wall, which was holding her up much better than she thought her legs would. Slowly with trembling fingers, she began to look at each picture.

The memory of that wonderful day returned to her, and as she looked at Darren—his well-muscled, shirtless body awash with the glow of the sun—she could almost make believe that everything was all right, and that the past days had been nothing more than a bad dream.

But the nightmare took on reality when the mists cleared from her eyes. She stared at the next photograph of Darren and felt a lump grow in her throat. She had captured the intense concentration of the artist at work. The photograph showed his face in full profile; his short, almost midnight-dark beard stood out in contrast to his tanned face.

"Why can't you see things from my point of view?" she asked Darren's face.

Why can't you see them from mine? the photograph seemed to whisper back at her. Although she swore that it was Darren's voice she heard in her ears, she knew it was only her thoughts, swiftly changing to direct the other side of the issue at her—the side she had always ignored.

I never ignored it! she protested silently, remembering the vast amount of research she had undertaken to find the best way to design the proposed community. But the random, unexpected thoughts had sewn a seed of doubt in her mind, stirring an unsolvable paradox.

Under the strain of her thoughts, Lea returned to the hotel suite, and, once inside, found Jason smiling proudly at her. "Done!" he declared as he held up the finished illustration of Stetman's valley.

Lea's eyes traced across it, searching for any hidden flaw. She found none, and slowly smiled at Jason. "It's magnificent."

"Yes it is, isn't it?" the artist responded good-naturedly.

"What time is it?" she asked.

Jason looked at his watch. "One. Don't you think you should get a watch?" he asked.

"I had one once," she replied absently, not seeing the puzzled look Jason gave her. "Are there any protective tubes around?"

Again, puzzled by her question, Jason stared at her. "For what?"

"I want to go to the valley, and I want to bring the drawing with me."

"Oh..." Jason said, not quite thrilled with her plans to take his work into the field. But, before he could protest her actions, she held up a conciliatory hand.

"I'll be careful," she promised as she went to the blue prints, slipped them out of the case, and held the empty tube out to Jason. "I promise I'll take care of it."

Reluctantly, Jason rolled the finished drawing and slipped it into the heavy cardboard sleeve. When he handed it to her, Lea smiled at him.

"Thank you," she said, turning to leave.

"Lea?" Pausing, Lea looked back at Jason. "Things will work out. The idea and plans are too good to be stopped, and the time is right for you!"

Lea held Jason's confident gaze for several seconds. "If I'm not back when Alicia returns with the copies, thank her for me, and tell her to have a nice Sunday off, and that I'll see her on Monday."

And then Lea left to drive to Stetman's valley, and try to settle her mind and regain the purpose that had been so dominant a force in her life, and that had kept her going for so long.

Chapter Thirteen

Darren turned over the last page of Lea's proposal and leaned back. Ever since waking in the Land Rover that morning, his mind had seemed to be clearer than it had been in days. Perhaps, he felt, it was because of the crisp, clean air, along with the absence of anything man-made, that had worked the magic upon his mind.

Whatever it was, Darren appreciated the freedom from his anger and hurt while he read the pages that Lea had given him. He had taken special care in his reading, especially whenever he found yellow highlighted sections.

He had read and reread several parts of the proposal for the community, and had been surprised to find himself nodding in agreement with many of the innovations Lea was intending to use.

But on the whole, Darren still believed that no matter how innovative, or how carefully everything was supposed to be done, the construction, and the very fact that people would inhabit what was now free land that animals and birds lived upon, would do irrevocable harm.

That space would be taken from the animals, and the fact that the natural flow of water—although the plans called for no change—would most likely be disturbed would interrupt the life cycles and patterns that had been in existence for untold hundreds of years.

She was wrong! Darren repeated the silent litany to himself. But he realized that Lea Graham was not as evil as he had been making himself believe.

What she was endeavoring to do with the valley was something he had wanted to see done for a long time, Darren admitted. Yet, because it was untried and unproven, he did not want it to take place in Stetman's valley.

The phone rang, jarring him back to reality. Standing, Darren crossed the white tile floor of the kitchen and answered the call brusquely.

"You're in a good mood," Andrew Blake said.

"Good enough," Darren replied, softening his voice.

"Any luck with the Graham woman yet?"

Darren didn't reply right away. His eyes went to the stack of papers he'd just finished reading. In his ears, he heard Lea's throaty voice reach out toward him in a collage of last night's heated confrontation.

I tried to tell you, but you wouldn't let me...Only yours is a perfect vision; only something that the great Darren Laird can see, can create, is good...Love! You don't know the meaning of the word!

When Darren managed to shake Lea's voice from his ears, he took a deep breath and spoke. "Not yet," he told Andrew, not knowing why he was lying.

"Well, keep trying," Andrew said.

"I will," Darren replied in a low voice, hanging up without bothering to say good-bye.

Why did I do that? he wondered as the earlier crystal-clearness of his thoughts became blurred. He tried to ignore the things that rose sharply upward in his mind but could not. He remembered the day they had watched the eagle, and the heated argument that they'd had. He thought about it carefully, doing his best to reconstruct their every word and gesture.

But in that, Darren failed. Yet, for the first time since that day, he was aware of another factor. They were supposed to have gone out to dinner that night. Lea's arrival at his house in the morning had surprised him. *Had she really come to tell me about herself?*

Then why didn't she? But Darren realized he had been too excited about being able to sketch the eagle, and had never given her a chance to explain her sudden appearance.

But she'd had the whole day! Almost angrily, Darren stalked out of the house, and went to his studio.

Belatedly, he realized he hadn't bothered to clean his brushes the previous night.

Shrugging, Darren took the three brushes and put them into paint thinner; then he picked up four clean brushes. *It's time*, he told himself. *Time to finish and put it to rest.*

The compulsion that had driven him to do this particular painting had not abated in the least. The closer it came to completion, the more Darren hoped that when he put his final brushstroke to it, he would be able to rid himself of his need to continually look at Lea's face.

Working with single-minded determination, Darren would not let his eyes drift to Lea's face; rather, he focused on the eagle as he gave it life with the tawny golden colors from his palette.

His concentration was total, as it usually was when he lost himself within his work. And, when he finally added the one small dab of pure gold to the eagle's head, he exhaled loudly and stepped back, not realizing that three hours had disappeared from the day.

After studying the painting, he slowly nodded his head and approached it again. He opened a new tube of paint and spread a small amount on the palette. Lifting the only brush he had not yet used, he dipped its almost spear-like bristle tip into the paint, and then signed his name on the lower right-hand corner.

When he finished, he carried the painting to the far wall and hung it on two nails, already set in the wall, where it would stay until the surface was dry enough to be touched.

And then? he asked himself. But he knew the answer. This painting would never go to the gallery. He would keep it himself, stored away from any and all eyes.

Darren walked slowly back to his work area, a feeling of heaviness descending on him. Usually, when he finished a painting, he felt lighthearted and sometimes even surprised at his ability to transform a piece of inanimate canvas into a living image of what his mind's eye had visualized. Usually, his spirits were uplifted by what he had created; but not this time.

As he reached for the brushes, his hands stopped midway. Turning slowly, he looked back at the painting. From this distance, everything about it was changed.

The valley did not show as fully as it did close up, and the only two things that really stood out were the golden eagle and Lea's face.

Her eyes seemed to be on him rather than on the eagle. He was suddenly feeling the way her eyes had caressed him so freely when they had been together and had fallen so deeply in love.

He saw within the eyes he had painted the same gentle warmth that had turned to burning passion, calling out to him in need and love. Try as he might, he could not make the eyes change into those of the cold, calculating woman he wanted to believe Lea was.

Anger welled up in him, but abated as quickly as it had formed. Confusion tried to claim his thoughts, but he did not allow that to happen. He willed his mind to clear, and then he finally picked up the brushes and cleaned them. When that task was done, he glanced at the painting.

Once more, the painting seemed to change before his eyes. Lea's eyes, glowing with green and golden flecks, pierced him with an accusatory stare. He saw the pity within them that had been there last night, moments before she had left. He remembered, all too well, her words to him about his own fears he had transferred to her. He had refused to listen to them last night, but he had no choice now.

In that suspended moment of ethereal time, he knew that she truly did love him, even as he loved her; but he understood that their love was doomed because of who they were, and what each had to do.

Let her go, he advised himself. But his eyes returned to the painting, and he knew he could not let her go, nor would the haunting specter of her eyes leave him. Although his own stubborn pride, strengthened by his willpower, tried to rise to his aid, he knew he had only one option left.

He must go to her and show her, using the love that seemed never to fade, that what she was doing was wrong.

Five minutes later, with the sun an hour past its zenith, Darren drove into Santa Fe. On the seat next to him was Lea's proposal.

Lea sat on the rocks above the valley. Tears flowed unashamedly from her eyes. She thought of all the years she had worked to reach this very point in her life; of the commitments she had willingly accepted; and of the hidden and guiding force that was part of her goals— her mother's unfulfilled and unacknowledged dreams. Yet the empty feeling within her heart reminded her of just how much she had given up to see the project succeed.

"But I didn't give him up," she whispered to the tall pine trees far below, "he gave me up."

The cardboard tube with the drawing of the valley was next to her, and as she tried to control her emotions, she reached down and picked it up. Before taking the drawing out of the tube, she remembered her promise to Jason and, standing up, moved to the spot where she had already spread a blanket.

As she withdrew the drawing, she tried to clear her eyes. But the previous night's confrontation still remained strong in her mind; and the unforgiving way Darren had reacted to her request that he read the proposal was like a fist striking her in the heart.

Carefully, she opened the drawing wide. The breeze tugged at the paper, but she held it steady and looked at Jason's rendition of the project. Then she lowered it and, with the illustrated image still strong in her mind, she looked down.

Suddenly she was seeing the finished project, hearing the happy sounds of the people who lived there, and feeling a sense of accomplishment.

Closing her eyes, Lea wiped the vision from her consciousness. There were still far too many pitfalls before her, for her to believe it would be that simple to complete the work.

Lea sighed and shook her head, thinking of the many and rapid changes that had marked her life during the past two weeks.

Without wanting it to happen, Lea remembered the time she had spent with Darren. The hours that they had driven along the highways and unpaved side roads, while he pointed out the sights and spoke of his need to paint the magnificent countryside.

Her memories attacked her relentlessly, as nothing had ever done before. Their power lashed out at her, washing over her, making her tremble with a loss that overwhelmed her and made her feel insignificant.

She saw again the last night that she and Darren had been together. She felt the emotions and the love that had compelled her to be with Darren, to taste the salty sweetness of his skin, and feel the taut muscles of his back as he carried her to the very heights of love. "I love you, Darren," she whispered hopelessly.

Her hands shook under the force of the memories, and Lea, taking deep, shuddering breaths, forced herself to stop thinking of anything. After several eternal moments, she had regained a small degree of control over her vacillating emotions.

Finally, Lea raised the drawing and tried to study it, but failed. Giving up for the moment, she rolled it tightly. But, before she could replace it within the tube, she heard footsteps approaching behind her.

When she turned, her hand flew to her mouth, but it was too late to stop her startled cry from escaping.

Darren had parked in the hotel's lot and gone directly to Lea's suite. The determination to make her see what he felt and saw had guided his feet. He'd knocked hard, and a moment later the door had opened to reveal a man of about the same age as Darren.

"Is Lea here?" he'd asked.

Jason had recognized Darren from publicity photos in the art magazines he read. "Can I help you, Mr. Laird? My name is Jason Browning."

Although surprised that the stranger knew him, Darren had not let that fact show on his face. "Where is she?" he'd demanded as he rudely pushed into the suite.

"Out," Jason had replied, "like you'll be in five seconds!"

Darren had shrugged at the anger in the man's face. "Take it easy," he told Jason as he held out the proposal. "Where do you want this?" Before Jason had replied, Darren had turned and put the bundle of papers on the desk.

When that was done, Darren had looked around the suite. Spotting the tilted drawing table, and the work sitting on it, he'd ignored Jason and gone over to it.

"Mr. Laird, that's not for public viewing," Jason had stated.

Darren had glanced at the man. "It will be when you file."

"But until then it's not. Don't make me call security."

Darren had laughed. "What security? This is Santa Fe, not the big city." Before Jason's anger had grown more intense, Darren had spoken again. "Relax," he'd commanded, "I'm not the enemy...today." Turning back to the drawing, Darren had studied it carefully with his trained eyes. When he'd finished, he'd turned to Jason. "Yours?" he'd asked.

Jason had nodded.

"Why are you wasting your talent on this drivel? The drawing shows me that you have a good deal of talent. You could be a real artist."

"Like you?" Jason had said, his brown eyes hardening. "Or is seeing only one side of an issue the requirement for success? No thank you, Mr. Laird. I happen to love what I do, and if you think that I'm wasting my talent because I'm an architectural renderer, that's your problem, not mine."

Darren had held the man's heated stare for several more seconds before he'd finally spoken. His voice had been low, but his words had carried clearly in the air between them.

"My apologies, Mr. Browning. I did not intend to offend you."

"But you seem to have that habit, don't you?" Jason had asked.

Darren had shaken his head slowly, refusing to be baited. "Why are you picking a fight with me? It's not because I was rude to you just now."

"That helped. No, it's because of the way you treated Lea Graham."

Darren had stared at him, not quite sure what he meant by his statement. "We're on opposite sides of a fight. How else am I supposed to treat her? Am I supposed to lie down and let her, and the company both of you work for, just steam-roll over me like you intend to do to the valley?"

"Is that what you're here about?" Jason had asked, his voice sharp. "Or is there more? Lea told me that you mean a great deal to her. Is that also as one-sided as the way you feel about any change in the valley?"

Darren had refused to rise to the bait. "That is none of your business."

"I'm afraid you're wrong again. Lea is my friend, and she's a damned good person. She's spent two solid years working on this project. She gave up everything in her life to make this project a success, so that perhaps one day in the future people will realize they don't have to destroy the environment to live comfortably. And, dammit, I don't think you have the right to use the power of your name to hurt her, and take advantage of the way she feels about you to destroy her dreams!"

"And you think that's what I'm doing?" he'd asked in a low voice.

"It sure seems like it to me," Jason had stated, his tone as unyielding as ever.

Under the twin assaults of the thoughts that had brought him to this room and Jason's strongly worded accusations, Darren had begun to understand a little more of what had been compelling him to fight this battle.

"Perhaps you're right," he'd said to Jason, his eyes fixed on the other man's. Then he'd taken a deep breath. "Where is she? I want to speak to her."

A half hour later, Darren had driven along the up-grade toward the spot where he hoped he would find Lea. When he'd seen her car, his breath had eased softly through his lips. When he'd pulled to a halt next to her car, he'd shut the ignition off, but hadn't left the vehicle.

Darren's hands returned to the steering wheel and gripped it hard; his knuckles had turned a pale white. Staring out through the windshield, he'd seen nothing. Finally, after taking a long breath, Darren had released his hold on the steering wheel and left the Land Rover.

The instant he'd crested the hilltop, he'd stopped. Standing not twenty-five feet away, with her back to him, had been Lea. Her shining sable hair had been tossed randomly about by the ever-present breezes; her clothing had been pressed against her body by the same breezes. She'd stood so still that he couldn't make himself go to her yet; instead, he'd continued to gaze at her, tracing the smooth curves of her body while she lowered the large paper in her hands.

When she'd begun to roll the drawing up, he had stepped forward. The sound of his boots on the rocky earth had seemed very loud in the gentle quiet of the hilltop.

When he was close to her, he'd seen her stiffen and turn; the back of the hand holding the rolled drawing had flown to her mouth, unable to stop her startled cry from reaching his ears.

"Hello Lea," he whispered.

"Why won't you leave me alone?" she asked in an unsteady voice after lowering her hand. Her body still felt the effects of her earlier memories, and Darren's sudden appearance attacked her harshly and brought back all the memories she had just ridden herself of.

"Because I can't. Because I need to talk with you," he admitted.

"*With* me, or *at* me?" she challenged, her voice growing strong as she fought against the conflicting emotions that told her to hate him, and told her to love him.

"Will you let me speak?" Darren asked as he gazed at her face, seeing the reflection of her pain become so suddenly apparent on her features.

"Why? So you can tell me how terrible I am again? So you can point out all the places that you claim I'll rape?" she asked, her voice rising sharply as she swung her arm outward and, using the cardboard tube, pointed toward the valley.

Darren held her stare without blinking. His hands were balled into fists at his sides, and his breathing was tight within his chest. "No, to tell you how terrible I am."

Lea blinked several times. Her arm was still stretched out, pointing at the valley. She was frozen to the spot, suspended in time as she watched him. Then her heart began to pound loudly, and her mind spun madly as she finally lowered her arm.

Lea did not move toward him; she stood her ground, fighting the swelling of her heart, silently praying that this was not some game he was playing to break down her barriers and defeat her.

Darren studied the defensive stiffness of her body, noting the doubt that so clearly showed on her face. "We found something very special when we met," he began, his voice hoarse with emotion, "but we lost it."

"We?" Lea challenged, speaking for the first time since his admission.

"We," he repeated. "Any relationship has to take into consideration both people. Lea, I was wrong in the way I reacted to you; you were right about my fears. I have been hurt before, by someone who used me. And your own deception hurt me even more."

"My deception, or your unwillingness to let me tell you about myself?" she asked, his words once again striking deeply into her heart. "How can you be so narrow—"

"Let me finish, Lea, I need to do this," he said before she could go on. "I know now that I really didn't give you much of a chance to explain to me about yourself. But I also believed that if you had really wanted to tell me, you would have found a way." Pausing, Darren moistened his lips before continuing. "Then I realized that if you had told me the truth, I would have reacted exactly the way I ultimately did react."

Silence fell suddenly, and Lea's breathing stopped with his confession. Hope struggled to the forefront of her thoughts, but Lea would not accept it, not yet.

"I love you, and I can say this because I know it's true," Darren told her. "But that doesn't change the fact that I hate what you're going to do to the valley. My whole life has been directed to preserving nature. At first it was only on canvas, but in the last few years, I've worked hard to do more than just paint what is around us.

"I can't stop that now—not unless I know that whatever is going to be done will not destroy the land. I will fight you, Lea, as a naturalist fighting someone who is trying to change the land, but I won't fight you emotionally. I love you, and I want to share more than just a battle with you."

Lea shook her head, trying to force his unsettling words into some order that she could understand. Her heart, which had sped up when he told her that he loved her, had almost stopped when he promised that he would not stop fighting her.

"Darren, I've loved you since the first moment I saw you. I've never before felt the emotions that come to life when I'm with you. When we're together, I can almost believe that nothing can go wrong in the world. But that's fantasy, not real life."

Pausing, she gazed at him, almost swaying under the rushing warmth of the memory of when they had held each other so closely. "I love you," she repeated, her voice growing thick as her tone filled with sadness, "but it doesn't make any difference."

"It has to," Darren stated.

Lea watched Darren, and saw the interplay of muscles in his cheeks from the pressure of his tightly clamped teeth. The breeze tousled his dark hair and tugged at his shirt. For just a moment, as he stood tensely on the hilltop, Darren's silhouette reminded her of the way he had looked when he'd stood above her, outlined by the fire, moments before they'd made love that long-ago night.

"How can our love withstand beliefs that are so opposite? You're a great artist, Darren, and you transform your beliefs into magnificent paintings. I would never ask you to give up what you believe in, your life's work."

Fighting to control her emotions, which threatened to take away her ability to speak, Lea carefully formed her next statement. "The only way we can have a life together is if I give up what I do, if I turn my back on my career and the dreams I've spent my whole life working toward. And if I do that, will I still be the same person you fell in love with? What kind of a future will we have?"

"A better one than being alone," Darren whispered. His words, so softly spoken, were carried to Lea on the mountain breezes that continued to caress her face.

Closing her eyes, Lea tried once again to make him see the hopelessness of the situation. "This isn't a Cary Grant–Doris Day movie. This is reality!" she stated bluntly, refusing to give in to the pleas of her heart, which cried out for her to go to him and be held by his strong arms and to taste the warmth and sweetness of his mouth.

"Lea—"

"No! We can't be enemies fighting during the day and then making love at night. I can't shed my feelings and leave them in the office at the end of the day. My work, like yours, is a part of me. It wouldn't work."

Instead of replying, Darren started toward her. He saw her tense again and take a hesitant step back. But she stopped suddenly, her eyes locking with his as he approached.

He swept his gaze across her face, realizing that her green-flecked eyes were no longer those of the haunting image that had plagued him in the studio, but the real and bottomless wells that led to her inner being.

Slowly, as if time itself stopped, Darren took her in his arms. Lea's arms hung at her side; one hand held the empty tube, the other the drawing. Her body went limp, but Darren drew her firmly to him, covering her lips with his and kissing her deeply.

The embrace lasted for an eternity, and while Darren's mouth worked gently upon Lea's, all the love she had for him rose powerfully to attack her senses and make her doubt what she had just told him.

The kiss ended slowly and, as Darren drew away, he spoke. "Why can't it work?" he asked, his voice laden with love and need.

"Darren—" But before she could again deny what he was saying, and what her heart was pleading for, his mouth returned to hers to rekindle the flames she had never quite been able to extinguish from her memory, or her body.

This kiss, too, lasted an eternity, and when it ended, her blood was pounding loudly in her ears. But it was not able to drown Darren's next remark.

"We can try," he stated. "We *have* to try," he added.

The world spun madly about Lea, and her only anchor was Darren's hands on her arms. She looked into the deep, blue-gray depths of his eyes and saw that he believed what he said. She found that the hopes she had been holding back were still with her, crying out to be set free.

"I...I'm afraid to try," she whispered. "And I'm afraid not to."

Darren bent, and again covered her lips as Lea dropped the drawing and the tube and her arms went around him. They clung together desperately while their needs built and their desires sprang free.

They sank slowly to the blanket, lost within the kiss. When they were resting upon the solid ground, their mouths still together, their hands reacquainting themselves with the feel of each other's body, Lea knew that she was helpless to fight him any longer.

But when Darren laid her down on the blanket, and then turned them both on their sides, he flinched.

"What?" she asked, concerned, and ignoring the racing of her pulse and the desires that made her want to pull him back to her.

Darren sat up and pulled the hard cardboard tube from under him. Then he smiled at her, shook his head and reached for the rolled-up drawing. But, as his fingers went around it and he started to put it into the tube, he stopped, and began to unroll it.

Lea's breath caught. The speeding flow of her blood stopped and the delicious feeling of warmth and butterflies within her stomach vanished. Her mind froze as the sudden rising of her hopes, that somehow they would surmount their different ideologies, was shattered anew. She knew that the moment he opened the drawing, the love they were trying to re-establish would be doomed by Darren's seeing how Lea actually planned to change the valley.

Still lying back on the blanket, Lea would not look at his face, and stared only at his hands as they carefully unrolled the drawing. She waited for what seemed to be forever, the tension racing almost painfully through her, until she could no longer stand it, and sat up.

Warily, she looked at his face and saw that he was studying the large drawing very carefully; but she could read nothing on his face.

Finally, Darren lowered the drawing and looked at Lea. "Last night, when you came to the studio and brought me your proposal, you told me about the community you envisioned for the valley, which would use the land rather than abuse it." As Darren spoke, his eyes grew distant and Lea was afraid that she was about to lose him for good.

"When you talked about the older, retired people living with the younger ones, it made me think about how much society has changed. Where families once cared for the older members, they now send them off to die elsewhere, as if they had served their purpose and were of no more use. I've always believed that was wrong, that it deprived children of the knowledge of where they really came from, and of having someone around whom they could turn to when their parents were not around."

Darren blinked his eyes, and then refocused on Lea. He smiled gently, almost apologetically. "I didn't mean to go off on a tangent," he told her. "But, even after you tried to explain your ideas to me, I didn't really understand them. I read your proposal, especially the parts you marked, and I understood a little more of what you want to do. But—"

The tension that had been holding Lea prisoner had slowly abated as he spoke, and Lea was almost believing that he had changed his mind, until he added that final word.

"But you won't stop trying to prevent the construction," she finished for him.

Darren stared at her, his mouth drawn into a tight line. "Last night you accused me of not letting you explain yourself. Are you going to do the same to me?"

Lea caught her lower lip between her teeth and slowly shook her head.

"Good! But...as I was saying, I couldn't even begin to imagine what you envisioned for the valley when you spoke to me. The proposal helped a little, but the technical language and descriptions were almost impossible for me to decipher into something I could visualize.

"Lea, I'm an artist. I can translate emotions to canvas, I can look at a scene and see the beauty or the wrongness in it. But I can't see that in a bunch of words. However," Darren said in a stronger voice as he raised Jason's rendition of the valley, "I can see what you were trying to say in this!" Then Darren smiled.

Lea saw the change come over his face, and the sinking sensation of loss was suspended as she tried to figure out what he was really telling her.

"This is not bad at all," Darren said, shifting and laying the drawing down between them on the blanket. His passion was temporarily set aside as one long, slim finger darted out to hover about a group of houses near one valley slope.

"If you set each of these houses back another twenty feet, they would blend in better with the slopes. And these three buildings," he questioned as his finger darted toward the trio of three-story buildings that Lea had worked so hard to stop from standing out too blatantly, "what are they?"

"Office buildings," she told him.

Darren shook his head slowly. "You tried too hard to make them look like houses. Instead, you could use the same idea as you did with these solar panels," he told her, pointing to Jason's elaborately camouflaged notch in the valley walls.

"Instead of using regular windows, use reflective glass panels. Although it's stark and way out of character for the valley, if you transplant some giant oaks and pines, and put them around the buildings, the windows will magnify the trees and help to hide the way the buildings stand out. And," he continued, throwing himself completely into Lea's concept of the valley, "since you'll be recycling the waste water and purifying it, the additional irrigation from that source will insure the larger trees' survival."

Lea stared at him as he continued to talk, her mind crazily adrift at this totally unexpected change in him. Her heart filled with love and hope, but the warning that was still strong in her mind made her temper her excitement with caution.

Slowly, she lifted her hand and placed a finger across his lips. Darren stopped talking then and looked at her, his eyebrows arched in question.

"Why? Why are you telling me this? Are you not going to fight me anymore?"

Darren caught her hand in his and turned it palm up. He returned it to his mouth, and kissed the soft warm skin. Then, still holding her hand tightly, he shook his head. "That depends on you. Can you really do what you think you can? Can you maintain the environment and not disrupt the life cycles except for construction?"

"I think I can," Lea whispered, ignoring the flaring heat that was racing up her arm, caused by his hand holding hers.

"You'd better do more than just think you can. I'll get the rest of the league to agree to let the construction go on—"

"Darren," Lea began, but he shook his head quickly.

"As long as we're allowed to be a part of it. To inspect the site regularly, and to insure that the construction follows your plans."

Lea blinked away the emotional tears that Darren's words brought up, and moistened her lips with the tip of her tongue. But before she could speak, Darren went on.

"If there are any infractions, or any hidden construction, the deal is off and we'll fight you until hell freezes over. I promise you that," he said, his face and voice backing the fierceness of his promise.

"I...I think I can get the board to agree on that," she said in a low voice. She was sure that she would be able to work out what he wanted with Mr. Lansing and the board of directors. She knew they would think it worth the expense to avoid a public confrontation with the ecology group, and she was also sure that the publicity resulting from their working together would be of even greater help to the project, and to the future of projects like hers.

"There's one other thing," Darren said a moment later.

"What?" Lea asked, afraid that it would be the one thing she could not promise.

"That you agree to marry me."

"Oh...Darren," she whispered even as she leaned toward him. They kissed, but suddenly, with a strange wrenching in her mind, Lea was no longer on the valley's rim, but had been transported back in time to her mother's office. She saw her mother bent over the drafting table; her father was standing next to her. Then her mother sat straight and looked at her. A slow smile spread across Janice Graham's features as both she and her husband nodded to Lea, pride showing plainly on their faces.

Then Lea opened her eyes and drew back from Darren. "Yes, my love, I will marry you."

READERS' COMMENTS ON SILHOUETTE SPECIAL EDITIONS:

"I just finished reading the first six Silhouette Special Edition Books and I had to take the opportunity to write you and tell you how much I enjoyed them. I enjoyed all the authors in this series. Best wishes on your Silhouette Special Editions line and many thanks."

—B.H.*, Jackson, OH

"The Special Editions are really special and I enjoyed them very much! I am looking forward to next month's books."

—R.M.W.*, Melbourne, FL

"I've just finished reading four of your first six Special Editions and I enjoyed them very much. I like the more sensual detail and longer stories. I will look forward each month to your new Special Editions."

—L.S.*, Visalia, CA

"Silhouette Special Editions are — 1.) Superb! 2.) Great! 3.) Delicious! 4.) Fantastic! . . . Did I leave anything out? These are books that an adult woman can read . . . I love them!"

—H.C.*, Monterey Park, CA

*names available on request